The Power of Touch

Barry —
Thank you for
Being A
Dear
Friend!

JIM HAYDEN

While the cases are based on real life events, the names, dates, businesses, places, locations, people, and details, etc. have been changed, invented and altered to the point that the reader should consider this book nothing more than a work of literature. Any reference or connection to any person, place, location, etc. to actual persons, living or dead is purely coincidental as details are either the product of the author's imagination or have been used in a fictitious manner. Furthermore, all healing and medical information contained in this book is for entertainment purposes only. The reader should always consult a medical professional with respect to any physical or emotional symptoms that may require diagnosis or medical attention. Please do not attempt self treatment of an emotional, medical, or any other health related problem without consulting a qualified health care professional.

ACKNOWLEDGMENTS

I want to personally thank the people who helped bring this publication to light. Paul Thayer, Susan Ball, and Stephanie Elliot – key players who had a hand in making this story so much better. And Darleen Whitworth, whose talent with artwork is out of this world. Most importantly, I want to thank Cecilia Marie for her unwavering support throughout this writing. She was my 'right hand man' from start to finish. I owe so much to all of you. Thank you.

Oftentimes, the actions or words of an emergency medical service provider can seem heartless or even cruel. I believe it is more of a defense mechanism than anything else – a protective barrier designed to keep them separated from the emotional challenge of witnessing another human's suffering. Tragedies, such as these depicted in this writing, must have a deplorable emotional impact for those who work in emergency medical services. We must never forget the dire circumstances they oftentimes find themselves in. The tragedies they face. The life and death decisions they might be required to make. To these men and women, we owe our deepest gratitude.

ONE

July 30, 1988 – 4:39 PM

Whooort! Whooort! Whooort! Whooort!

"Channel Two. EMS assignment. Drowning. Sixty-Eight-Ten North Eighteenth Avenue. Engine Twelve," a tinny female voice announces from the little black scanner.

The telephone rings. Trevor runs to the black rectangular box that hangs on the wall and lifts the receiver. "Station Eleven!"

I tense with a thought. *We're getting this one.*

I sit on the sofa – chin on the palm of my hand – anticipating the confirmation of that feeling.

"Seventeen! Code three!" Trevor shouts. "That's us, Jimmy."

I bolt from the sofa and join my partner. Our

race against time begins as we descend the stairway of the narrow hall toward Ambulance Seventeen, our mindset shifting to one sole focus – to save a life.

My partner climbs into the driver's side of the cab, slots the key and starts the engine. I pull myself into the passenger's seat. Code three means lights and sirens. I flip the switch to sound the alarm.

The ambulance speeds out of the station into the treacherous sunlight of a scorching hot summer afternoon. Heading westbound on Bethany Home Road, I think of how drownings have become common here in Phoenix, and my mind folds into the possibilities of what might be waiting for us.

Images of the last drowning flash to my mind. I shudder with the memory.

I have to remember to take my boots off this time.

TWO

July 30, 1988 – 4:50 PM

Pressing his foot on the pedal, Trevor accelerates, barreling the ambulance toward Eighteenth Avenue. Lights strobe and sirens blare as we dodge traffic.

We turn southbound onto Eighteenth Avenue. A row of houses painted in a variety of colors line both sides of a short and narrow street. Chain link fencing defines property lines where dried Bermuda grass and dusty palm trees grace small patches of land, and nosy neighbors vie for opportunities to see what's causing the commotion.

I spot the large red fire truck as I naturally search for a place to park. A smattering of older vehicles line the curb.

"I don't see a place, Jimmy."

"There's space behind the fire truck. Park there."

Trevor pulls the ambulance around. Slams on the brakes.

Doors open, and we jump out. We gather our equipment from the back of the cab and run it through the driveway, past the red Chevy, through the back gate, into the yard where the pool occupies most of the landscape. I breathe in the chlorine that saturates the air.

Shouts thunder. Information flies. Hands work to pull supplies, wield equipment, and tend to the victim.

We advance to the emergency medical team that hovers over the body lying sprawled on the pool deck.

"Whada we got?"

Trevor and I nudge our way between firefighters who are frantically working to save that life.

Oh, my God. It's a kid.

I throw my airbag to the ground and crouch next to the boy, eyeing the dark blue lips that protrude glaringly. My stomach drops. Sorrow burns through me.

Trevor drops to his knees.

"Kid can't be more than three years old," I say.

We pull out our latex gloves and slip them over our hands, snapping the latex to ensure a good fit.

"How can anyone let something like this happen?" I say, speaking in low tones.

"I don't know, Jimmy."

Trevor shakes his head.

A surge of anger flashes through me.

Keep your emotions outta this, Hayden. Focus on the task at hand.

I glance at the fireman crouched on his knee. He's removing a bright orange mask from its packaging. The horrid stench of smelly plastic blends with the chlorine and settles in my mouth with a nasty aftertaste. The fireman places the device on the boy's face. Secures the bag valve mask tightly over the nose and mouth.

Another fireman performs artificial respiration, squeezing the bag valve mask, filling it with air. I know he's hoping it will be enough to get the child to breathe. We're all hoping.

I watch as a third firefighter swipes the boy's arm with an alcohol swab to prep it for the IV needle.

I absorb the scene before me. It seeps effortlessly into my emotional being — the way a desiccated sponge fills with water.

I can't stop it. The despair I hold in my belly folds into burning anger as I question the helplessness of a child who finds himself in a desperate situation, powerless to save himself, not even knowing how to try. Where is the caregiver to whom the innocent child places so much trust?

How could the caregiver let this happen? I can't understand the dynamics of this. And this time is no different than any other. Why do children who seem so innocent and trusting in nature have to be put through trauma like this? Why?

Trevor takes the cylinder of oxygen out of the air bag and nearly tosses it at me. I twist the valve to get the oxygen flowing then turn the other valve to monitor the flow. I take the tubing and quickly connect it to the bag valve mask. The firefighter monitors the boy.

"There's no pulse!" A fourth firefighter shouts.

"Start chest compressions!" Trevor yells.

The fourth firefighter shifts positions, placing the palm of his hand on the boy's chest, pressing while counting, "One compression, two compressions, three compressions, four compressions, five compressions, breathe."

The sequence continues.

Thump.....

Thump.....

Thump.....

The muffled sound attracts my attention. I glance around to see what's causing the distraction.

I catch a glimpse of her, the woman, standing to the side, sobbing uncontrollably as she rhythmically pounds her head against the wall. Her facial features – unrecognizable. She's a discombobulated mass of substance that has lost complete control of any element of self-containment. It's obvious to me that her pride is gone and that she doesn't care about anything other than saving her son.

That's got to be the mother.

A mental picture of me in her shoes forms in my mind.

A tinge of agony crawls through me.

KEEP THE EMOTION OUT OF IT!

I quickly turn my attention to the matter at hand.

"He's not responding!" yells the fireman who's checking the pulse. "Should we intubate here or scoop and run?"

"We don't have time to intubate," I say.

Moving quickly, the fireman scoops the child while another holds the bag valve mask in place. I carry the oxygen tank while we run the child to the back of the ambulance. Trevor opens the doors to the wagon and pulls the gurney from the back. We place the child on the gurney, bring the sidebar to an upright position. Secure the middle, bottom and chest straps. I gaze at the boy. The view is unsettling – his tiny body lost in a shackle of cords.

We place the gurney into the ambulance. Two firemen flank the gurney. They continue to treat the boy.

Trevor runs to the front of the ambulance and climbs into the cab. I join the firemen in the back. He starts the engine, slams the gear shift into drive. I pull the wagon doors shut just before he drives off.

I don't know what to do. Should we go the

extra distance and get the boy to the trauma center or just rush him to the nearest hospital?

"Which hospital?" I ask.

Trauma centers are better equipped to handle situations where life hangs in the balance, but getting him to the nearest hospital would save time.

"This kid is asystole!" the fireman cries out. "We gotta get him to the nearest trauma center."

Oh, God. No heartbeat. "Let's get him to St. Rita's, then!"

The ambulance accelerates while we work to stabilize the boy.

Down local streets we fly. Lights strobe. Sirens blare. We brake at red lights. Clear the intersection. Regain speed. The roaring engine pulses through my veins.

Palm on the chest and pressing, "one compression, two compressions, three compressions, four compressions, five compressions," the fireman shouts. The ambulance yields to oncoming traffic and we slam into the front of the wagon.

"Breathe."

"Let's intubate!" another firemen yells. He removes the bright orange mask while another fireman takes the endotracheal tube, disconnects it from the bag valve mask, and inserts it quickly but gently into the child's nose, guiding it down – into the lungs. I pull out my stethoscope. Secure earpiece. Place the metal chest piece on the boy. I concentrate, listen intently for a gurgling, a murmur, anything that will tell me the tube is in the lung.

I move the chest piece. *There it is.* I breathe a sigh of relief, comforted in knowing that he is now receiving one hundred percent of oxygen. I take over chest compressions – counting, "one compression, two compressions, three compressions…"

We slam against the front of the wagon.

"Four compressions, five compressions…"

The ambulance regains speed. We resume our original positions.

"Breathe!" I yell.

A fireman checks once more for a pulse. He places his fingers on the carotid artery located in the neck just below the jaw line. He pauses. Moves his fingers to the groin where the femoral arteries are located. "Child's still asystole!"

"Keep trying!" I yell with a slight tremor in my tone.

Keep trying!

THREE

July 30, 1988 – 6:15 PM

An abrupt turn to the right takes us to the Emergency Trauma Center up ahead. Trevor hits the switch to kill the sirens as we pull into the drive. The ambulance brakes. Doors open, and with orchestrated speed we deliver the child to the emergency medical team who is anxiously awaiting our arrival.

Questions fly amid the chaos that is now the center of the emergency room. I trail the medical team that wheels the gurney to an open area. It's devoid of warmth – like a stainless steel chamber – complete with sterile equipment and expressions to match.

"What happened?" a doctor shouts while

approaching the child.

"Kid tried to get his ball out of the pool and fell in," a fireman responds.

"For how long?" the doctor yells, while pulling at the black tubing of the stethoscope he plugged into his ears.

"We don't know. Maybe ten, fifteen, minutes."

He places the metal chest piece onto the boy. A nurse takes the boy's blood pressure. Another checks the IV.

"How cold was the water?" He moves the chest piece around.

"Don't know. Maybe seventy, seventy-five degrees."

"Blood pressure's not registering," the nurse announces.

"There's no heartbeat," the doctor confirms.

"Changing out the IV!" another nurse shouts. "I need a syringe!"

She disengages the long clear tube from the IV bag that is half empty and attaches it to the new bag which is hanging on an apparatus that looks much like a moving coat rack made of steel. She checks the clear liquid seeping slowly into the boy's vein.

The doctor removes the chest piece and pulls a diagnostic penlight from his medical jacket. He examines the boy's eyes.

"Where's that syringe?" the nurse shouts.

She takes the syringe, raises it to the light, adjusts the contents. She inserts the needle into the secondary port and slowly injects the liquid into the tubing.

She eyes the respiratory therapist who is rushing toward her.

"Let's get him hooked up to our oxygen!" he yells.

The medical team works frantically to save the boy's life – each utilizing their skill set with a precision that would make an auto mechanic writhe with envy.

Lurking in the background, I stand watching, waiting... hoping for an opportunity to provide assistance.

Heck! What am I going to do?

I'm riddled with thought – wanting to know if the kid is going to make it.

I watch the medical team continue to work while my thoughts drift to a previous drowning – the visual imprint surfacing to my mind.

Yeah, I remember that one....

I was the only one who saw that kid floating in the water. He was unresponsive. I knew a few seconds could mean the difference between life and death, so I jumped into the pool, headed straight toward the kid when, suddenly, I realized the mistake I had made.

I remember becoming acutely aware of the cold water filling my work boots. My socks soaking in the water. My feet cold. Panic set in. I considered removing my boots but knew the kid could die in the time it would take to remove them. I kept them on, thinking that it shouldn't matter. I could make it. But the water added content. It was so difficult to force my way through the water. I remember the fear, resonating with the intensity of a tuning fork. It pulsed through my veins. But I kept moving, each step more agonizing than the one before. "Faster! Faster! I have to move faster!"

I felt as though I were encased in cement. Scenes from old-time mafia movies flashed in my mind as movement became more sluggish and water fought to hold me back. I reconsidered removing my boots, but I had to get to the kid.

I was frantic. With every fiber of my being, I forced my feet to move – terror shrieking through every muscle in my body. I shouldered the weight of the water. Legs straining, on fire with pain, propelling through the resistance – focused on getting to that kid.

I finally reached him, scooped him into my arms, raised him high while eyeing the distance to the deck. Didn't seem that far. I started across the pool when the bite of a searing burn crawled through my legs, spreading its fire through every muscle, every tendon, every nerve, as my work boots carried the weight of the water.

Wracked in guilt for being so stupid, I pressed through the resistance. Reaching the deck seemed an illusion, much like water that glimmers on the horizon of a faraway desert. Tears pricked my eyes.

Mucous trickled from my nose. Doubt was eating at me like a hungry dog. "I'm not going to make it!" kept running through my mind. Wincing in pain, I recharged my focus. I remember the "PUUUSHSHSH!" resounding in my head. My legs were writhing in agony, cramping from the strain. I finally reached the elusive deck and plopped the kid down. I grabbed the lip, tears spilling onto my cheeks, mucus lining my upper lip, my body quivering with complete exhaustion.

I hover in the memory.

"Hey, guy. We need to clean up," Trevor says.

I jump with the unexpected interruption.

"Yeah. Sure. What about the kid?" I ask.

"I don't know." Trevor shakes his head.

One of the best things about my relationship with Trevor is when emotion gets the better of either one of us, no words are necessary. We just know, and we let the one who is affected process the event. Sometimes it's a lengthy discussion. Sometimes it's a spaghetti dinner. We never belabor the point. We never examine it. We just do what it takes to shake it off.

We walk to the ambulance. Enter the patient's cabin where the child had been treated. There is little said between us as we each do our part with cleaning the equipment, discharging the garbage, securing supplies. I'm overwhelmed with thoughts of the boy. I want to know how he's doing, and the information isn't coming.

Trevor hauls himself into the driver's seat. With one hand on the wheel, he uses the other to turn the key already placed in the ignition. The engine roars to life. I clamber into the passenger's side and slam the door shut as Trevor pulls away.

We inch our way around the circular drive. The mother is standing at the end of the parking lot under an unlit street lamp. I can't help but stare at her. Her disheveled brown hair partially covers her swollen face. A white muscle tee shirt clings to her slender body. Her navy-blue knickers, heavily wrinkled. Her facial features, barely distinguishable – a sure sign of the depth of tears she has shed. There's no doubt in my mind that she has just been through the worst day of her life. She wears it unashamedly.

She lifts her gaze, pins my eyes. Her expression radiates sorrow. I absorb her agony. Lost in her experience, I now feel her worry, her bottomless grief, her fear of loss. It pours from her soul, filling me.

The ambulance creeps toward the stop sign that leads to the street. I'm suspended in time. The scene unfolds, inch by inch, frame by frame, moment by moment. I hold her gaze as I merge with her on a deep soulful level.

An intuitive force invades my body.

I cringe with a knowing.

My gaze travels to her lips, reads her message. "Thank you."

15

I nod. My mouth forms the words, but I don't speak them. I know she won't hear me. "You're welcome," I reply. I follow with a mock salute then turn my attention in another direction. I don't want her to know what I know, not now, not from me. I don't want to be the one to convey to her that her son has died.

I lower my head, rest in her pain, succumb to the heaviness billowing inside of me. A sudden desire to weep for her emerges. I want to cry out at the unfairness, scream that anyone should ever have to go through anything like this. I know the torture she will soon feel.

I lapse into a conscious coma, fold into the white noise of silence. I know to distance myself from the emotion of it, but sometimes that is easier said than done.

Trevor guides the ambulance – takes a circuitous route to the station.

Tears form and begin their descent, falling over the lower eyelid, onto my cheeks, leaving a gentle trail as they find their way onto my lap.

Why couldn't I have saved that kid?

Trevor remains silent.

I agonize over the kid's death, the vision of the mother seared in my mind.

"You okay, dude?" Trevor asks.

"Yeah, tough call. That's all."

Why is this bothering me so much?

"You wanna talk about it?"

"Nah. I'm good."
What's going on with me?
"You wanna go for some spaghetti?"

FOUR

July 31, 1988 – 9:10 AM

Back at the station, I awake from a restless night's sleep. The memory of the previous day's events lodged deeply within me.

I pull myself upright and throw my legs over the side of the steel framed bed. Images of the drowning surface. They gnaw at me like termites to wood.

I hurl myself off the thin twin mattress and shuffle into the tiny white bathroom. The mirror mounted on the medicine cabinet reveals the strain I hold in my face. I lean into the white pedestal sink. Peer at the reflection in the mirror.

God. I feel like I've been hit by a Mack truck.

I turn on the water, careful to balance the temperature so as to fill the room with steam.

Memories of the boy play like a motion picture in the back of my mind.

Forget about it.

I cup my hands to catch the running water and splash my face. I snatch a towel.

A final glance in the mirror reminds me that I need to change the white tee shirt and dark blue slacks I slept in last night, not to mention, shave.

I stare at the reflection.

Ah, screw it!

I exit the bathroom, plunk down on the bed, and slip into my black work boots. I don't bother to zipper them. I never do, unless I'm on a call.

Commotion from the break room seizes my attention.

I wonder what they're doing now.

I walk to the door. Step into the break room. I jump back to avoid the flying object that Al has tossed to Steve.

"You dawg!" Steve yells, chuckling as he hurls himself into the air to catch the little ball he tosses back to Al.

"Hey. Cut it out before somebody breaks something!" yells Bill who appears comfortably seated on the sofa. He's spraying whipped cream from a red and white container directly into his mouth.

"Hey, guys," I address them weakly as I hesitate to enter the room.

"Hey, Jimmy!" someone yells.

"Here!" shouts Al as he tosses the hacky sack over to Bill.

"Quit it." He laughs while whipped cream escapes wildly into the air. "Now look what you made me do." He scoops the creamy white mess that landed on the sofa and tosses it in Al's direction.

"B-i-i-i-i-l," whines Mark who gets hit with the whipped cream. "Leave me outta this." He chuckles as he throws the whipped cream back to Bill.

I make my way across the great room and head toward the kitchenette where coffee is brewing. *Emergency!* blares from the TV set. It's everyone's favorite show. The stories are ridiculous and never portray the real world of EMS protocol, but the crew enjoys criticizing the characters. It's always good for laughs, and it provides a background of entertainment we have become accustomed to.

An uneasiness rumbles inside of me.

I pour myself a cup of coffee, take a donut, and seat myself at a small round table. I sink into thought as I bite into the donut.

"Hey Buddy." Trevor pulls a chair from the table and takes a seat.

"Hey, Trevor."

"Rough day yesterday, huh?"

"Yeah."

I take a sip of coffee while observing the men in the room.

"Not much for talking today?"

"Not yet." I don an apologetic smile as I stare into the eyes of the man who is my best friend. His boyish features remind me of Opie, the kid from *The Andy Griffith Show.*

I read the understanding in Trevor's eyes. He picks up the newspaper and scans the headlines.

I turn my attention to Al and Steve who are tossing the hacky sack back and forth. Their animated play bothers me today. I watch with scornful eyes as my mind wanders.

I scrutinize Al. He's tall and lanky with short dark hair and black eyes. About forty years of age. Can be a real prick sometimes, but then I've seen times when he'd be on a call and break down. Steve can be a real prick, too. He's a lot like Al. Tall, slim but with a little more meat on his bones. Short brown hair. Brown eyes. Smart. I've watched him break down, too.

I take a bite of donut.

"Rampart. We have a patient in extreme pain. He's unconscious," the TV set announces.

Bouts of laughter dice the air.

"Oh. How can a patient be in extreme pain when he's unconscious?" Dennis says. My attention turns to Dennis. A different sort of guy. Likable by anybody's standards, but with a personality that makes it hard to take him seriously at times. About thirty years old. Never been married. Lots of gray coming through his hair. A little chubby. Round face. I can't take him today.

"Just like the time when they gave a patient a hundred liters of oxygen," says Joe.

Joe? He's just plain rude. A know-it-all. A bit rough around the edges. Stocky. Well built. Weighs

21

in about two hundred fifty pounds. All muscle. Italian style. Dark hair. Tanned skin. Always bragging on his daughter. We barely get along.

"That amount of oxygen would blow your head off," says Mark. Mark's young. Square jaw. Solid build. Strong. Likes to learn. In his early twenties.

"No shit," Joe chuckles.

I watch Bill squirt whipped cream into his mouth.

Seems so child-like. Bill's about five foot nine but looks more like five foot five because of his small frame. His blue eyes and blond hair compliment his boyish features. Reminds me of a ten-year-old kid.

I'm really not in the mood for the antics engaged with the day. My thoughts are on the loss of yesterday's child.

Yesterday's child. Like the title of a popular song. Weird.

"You know, I really feel sorry for her," I say.

"For who?" Trevor asks.

"The boy's mother."

"Why?"

"Because she now has to live with the guilt of irresponsibility."

"So?"

"So, imagine having that knowing drumming constantly in the back of your mind. Constantly reliving a horror you could have most likely prevented. It's a lifetime sentence that will haunt her for the rest of her life."

"Well, she deserves it."

"Maybe. That connection I felt with her yesterday was off the charts. I could feel her sorrow, feel her pain. I wanted to protect her. Shield her from the agony. It was tough."

Trevor shoots me a look of concern. "I think you're taking this a little too personal, Jimmy."

"Life doesn't seem fair sometimes." I take another bite of donut and follow it with a sip of coffee.

Trevor ignores me. Returns to his newspaper.

"You ever think about how cruel life can be, Trevor?"

"No. Why?"

"I don't know. Just thinking about it, I guess. How we become indifferent to people's suffering. How people can be so cruel to other people. People taking advantage. You know what I mean?"

"Yeah. Well. That's life," Trevor says.

"Remember the guy who claimed to have severe neck pain after being rear ended by another car?" I ask.

"No. Which one was that?"

"The one where there was no evidence of damage to his car, but he was crying about how severely injured his neck was."

"Oh. Yeah. I remember him. Joe was ragging on him. 'And you're telling me you have neck pain and want to go to the hospital?' Joe had a point, you

23

know. The guy was trying to take advantage of the system," Trevor says.

"Yeah. I know. But that's what I'm talking about. People taking advantage."

I take a bite of donut.

"And remember that time when we were called in the middle of the night to handle a lady with back pain?"

"Yeah. I remember her, too. Two o'clock in the morning. She had her back pain all day but waited till two o'clock in the morning to call us. I was pissed."

"Me too, but did it do any good to point that out to her? To point out that it was very inconsiderate of her to drag us out of bed at two o'clock in the morning when she could have called us earlier?"

"It was good for me. It was a stupid move for her."

"I hear ya, Trevor. But this is what we get paid for. And to be disrespectful and condescending isn't part of the job."

"You think I was disrespectful and condescending?" Trevor asks.

"Maybe."

Trevor huffs a laugh. "Well, Jimmy. Life is full of shitty conflicts. Get over it."

I glance over at the scanner, that little black box that screams life-threatening, life-saving messages to those of us whose job it is to listen to them.

I'm intrigued by the simplicity of the equipment

and the seriousness of its function, the mere fact that that little black box is purchased from a neighborhood Radio Shack and is no more complicated in its operation than to simply plug its cord into the wall.

I take a sip of coffee.

"I just think that there's too much suffering in the world. Too much."

"So, what are ya gonna do about it, Jimmy?"

I shrug diffidently.

FIVE

August 24, 1988 – 2:17 PM
Traveling westbound on Northern Avenue, we join the other two ambulances parked on the side of the road near 135th Avenue where the rollover has taken place. A red fire truck parks to block westbound traffic – not that there is any – but just in case. It's rare that anyone travels to the barren desert. There's no real life out this way save for the zoo. And even that's another thirty blocks or so down the road.

Trevor and I jump out of the cab and remove our gear from the back of the ambulance. I spot the white Plymouth Barracuda on the side of the road. It's perched on its roof. Hood crumpled. Doors crunched. The desert floor covered in splintered glass.

Trevor and I pass two crewmen transporting a patient to one of the ambulances as we approach the group of men standing in a tight circle. I squeeze my way in. On the ground lay a young girl. Couldn't be more than sixteen, maybe seventeen years of age. Her face is scraped but no real damage. No broken bones that I can see. Looks as if she's sleeping, but she's not. She's unconscious. Her shirt, ripped wide open. Her bra has been removed, her bare chest fully exposed. I tense with anger.

"Mark. Joe." I nod. "What's going on?"

"We're evaluating the depth of the impression the seat belt left on the girl's chest," says Joe.

"Really." I cast a look of indignation. Drop the airbag to the ground. "And it takes five of you to do that?"

I pull a blanket.

"Has anybody bothered to check vitals?" I ask as I glare at the men standing around.

"Well, we were checking the depth of the impression left by the seat belt," one of the firefighters says.

"You're a bunch of poor excuses for men, you know that?"

I throw the blanket over the girl's chest.

"What are ya, queer, Jimmy?" Joe asks.

"Yeah," I say with a sharp tone. "Get me the backboard, Mark. Let's get this kid to the hospital."

"I'll get the IV started," says Trevor.

I work on vitals.

"You other morons go find something to do," I say.

"Fuck you, Jimmy," Joe sneers.

"I bet you wish you could," I say through gritted teeth.

I turn my attention to the young girl.

"What's your problem, Jimmy?" Trevor asks while prepping the arm with an alcohol swab. "Ain't no harm in lookin'."

"She's in a life-threatening situation, Trevor. They're supposed to be saving her life, not checking out her tits." I take her blood pressure.

"You're taking this too seriously." Trevor inserts the needle. Applies the medical tape.

"It's a serious matter. Besides, I wouldn't want a bunch of horny bastards checking out my daughter's chest under any circumstance, no less this one." I peel her eyelids up.

"Let's just get her in the ambulance," Trevor says. "Let Joe take her."

"Joe?" I say incredulously as I pull back to eye Trevor.

"Yeah," Trevor says.

"I don't know. Do you think I can trust him not to fondle her?"

Trevor tosses me an expression of, "don't be ridiculous."

"Okay. Fine." I resign to the suggestion – watch as Joe and Mark approach to take her.

I'm fuming inside. Fuming at the insensitivity and complete disregard for human decency, human respect.

We head toward the ambulance.

"You drive, Trevor."

We jump into the cab. Trevor starts the engine.

"You're taking this too seriously, Jimmy."

"You already said that."

"Yeah, well, ease up, will ya?"

"Those fucking morons had no business undressing that girl. My God. She's just a kid. Freakin' child molesters."

"That's a bit strong, don't you think, Jim?"

"No."

"What would you do if it were your daughter?" I ask.

"I don't have a daughter, so I don't know." Trevor exhales a long stream of air. "You know, Jimmy, we are all fucking somebody's daughter. That's what we do. It's part of life. It's part of nature. I'm not saying what they did was right. All I'm saying is you really shouldn't take it so hard."

"You know what, Trevor? It reminds me of when I was a kid and my sister had to tell my parents that she was pregnant. She was fifteen years old at the time. She was horrified when they suggested she get an abortion. She refused to do it, and her nine months of pregnancy were riddled with constant judgment and comments on how irresponsible it was for her to keep the baby. God, I felt so sorry for her. I watched her suffer from the constant and endless barrage of scornful expressions every moment they laid eyes on her. I

29

just wanted to end it for her, you know? Stop the pain. Because I could feel it. I could feel what she was going through. The shame. The torment. All because she wanted to keep her baby."

"What's that got to do with viewing a naked chest?" Trevor asks.

"Human dignity. Respect. Decency. All of that. I'm just tired of people hurting on any level, and if that young girl knew she was being violated... How could she ever trust another EMT again?" I ask. "Just like my sister. How can she ever trust my parents again?"

The ambulance goes silent.

I reflect on the pain people experience every day. Situations people find themselves in where they are powerless. The pain and agony suffered just because they happen to be in the wrong place at the wrong time. The anger. The outrage by those afflicted. I think about people and life and how life affects people. And it doesn't matter how insignificant the experience might seem to another. It's the level of significance the victim attaches to the experience in that moment. It's what the victim perceives that matters.

"I care about people," I say.

"Why?"

"I don't really know. I just feel like there is a profound uniqueness in them. It interests me."

My observation is met with silence.

"Maybe it's because of the life challenges," I

continue. "How people respond to life challenges is educational to me. But that aside, I have a real compassion for people. It's buried way down deep in me, and I think it's time I start doing something about it."

"Like what?"

"Hell, I don't know. Like stopping horny bastards from staring at a kid's naked chest. Whaddya think?"

"I think you're a nut, Jimmy."

"Maybe I am." I smile.

SIX

Several months have passed since the drowning of the little boy. The events of that late afternoon are now a distant memory. Yet, the question of human suffering remains.

It's mid-morning. I'm at the station, sitting at the dinette table in the break room, reading the Sunday newspaper, enjoying a little bit of peace and quiet while I can. I take a sip of coffee.

"Whatcha doin'?"

I lift my gaze. It's Joe. He's standing in front of me with an air of arrogance on full display.

"What's it look like I'm doing?"

"You readin' about my daughter?" Joe asks.

"No. Why?"

"She's in the paper today. In the sports section. Her team won the championship for high school basketball."

A sardonic smile stretches across Joe's face. Makes my skin crawl.

"She makes me so proud of her," he adds.

"Cool," I say with disinterest.

"She's my pride and joy, ya know."

Joe takes a seat.

Steve approaches the table. "Talkin' about your daughter again?"

"Yeah. Her team won the championship in basketball last night. Get me a cup of coffee, will ya?"

"What school does she go to?" asks Steve.

"She's a senior at Xavier. She's graduating this year. You know she's my world."

Steve sets two cups of coffee on the table, one for Joe and one for himself. "Need a refill, Jimmy?"

"Naw. I'm good."

"My daughter. She's been accepted into Harvard. Wants to be a lawyer. A prosecutor to be more specific."

Al arrives. He turns the television channel to an episode of *Emergency!*

"Where does someone like you get the money to send his kid off to Harvard?" I ask.

"It's called, scholarship, Jimmy. My kid's that smart."

"She didn't get it from her father," I say with a chuckle.

"Screw you." Joe takes a sip of coffee.

"Why's she going to Harvard to be a prosecutor? Doesn't sound too smart to me – wasting a Harvard degree to become a prosecutor?" Steve asks.

"She's got bigger plans than that," says Joe with a demeaning tone.

Dennis drops by. "Whatcha guys talkin' about?" He gets himself a cup of coffee and seats himself at the table.

"My daughter," Joe says.

"How's she doing?" Dennis asks.

"I was just saying how she made the newspaper today. Her basketball team won a championship."

"Cool. Let me see."

I hand Dennis the sports section.

"Wow. She looks good. How old is she?" Dennis asks.

"Eighteen," Joe says. "She's a real beauty."

"Must take after her mother," Steve says.

"Yeah, well don't any of you be thinking you're going to be asking her for a date. If I catch any of you screwballs trying to lay a hand on her, I'll kill you myself."

I throw a glance at Steve and roll my eyes. "Oh, brother," I say under my breath.

"She's my life. Ain't nobody laying a hand on her unless I say so," Joe continues. "Nobody."

"Glad I ain't your kid," Steve says.

"Fuck off."

I chuckle.

A high-pitched shrill cuts into the exchange and

blasts against the backdrop of an episode of *Emergency!*

"Hot air balloon down. Interstate Thirteen and the Highway," the little black box squawks.

The telephone rings.

Bill runs to the phone. Lifts the receiver. "Station Eleven." He listens intently to the other end of the line.

"All units! Code three!" Bill shouts.

I rise from the table to join Trevor as the others pair up. We descend the stairway like an army of soldiers. Our program has shifted. Our focus is life. The battle is death. The race is against time.

Doors open. We climb into our ambulances.

"I'll drive," I say to Trevor.

*****

December 18, 1988 – 10:40 AM

Speeding down the highway, lights strobe, sirens blare. All four ambulances race to the scene.

Trevor turns the knob to the radio. Twisted Sister belts out lyrics to *We're Not Gonna Take It*. I turn up the volume.

"Must be pretty bad up there for all of us to be summoned," I yell at Trevor.

"I'd have to agree. What could have caused the balloon to go down?" Trevor asks.

"I don't know. Those balloons are operated by heat alone. Increase the heat and the balloon goes up. Decrease it, the balloon descends. And if the fire goes out, I understand the balloon is fairly easy to land."

"Yeah? How do you know this shit?"

"Was thinking about taking a hot air balloon ride some time ago. Did a little research."

I pull the zipper on my work boots.

"Could be a mid-air collision," I add.

Trevor arches a brow. "Really Jimmy?"

"Just sayin'."

"You're hilarious."

"Well, what else could it be?"

"Fuck if I know," Trevor says. "We'll find out when we get there."

Ambulances wheel onto an open tract of land large enough for a football field or two. Columns of thick black smoke cut into clear blue skies, rising from Bermuda grass that blankets the field. I press the gas pedal to the floorboard. Red fire trucks appear in the distance.

A firefighter runs toward us. I slam on the brakes bringing the ambulance to an abrupt halt. Other ambulances follow suit. Doors open, and Trevor and I quickly alight while others do the same. We collect our equipment and run to meet the fireman. The others run ahead.

"What happened?" I shout as we approach the firefighter.

"The pilot opened the parachute valve to complete his landing when a gust of wind caught the envelope, tipped the balloon, and dragged it about five hundred feet."

Walking briskly, we head to the scene. The fireman continues. "The balloon was at an angle, so the propane gas escaped the burner and spilled all over the field, and, of course, with the flame burning... well... you see the result." He points an arm at the raging fire. "The flame caught one of the passengers. Burned him pretty bad."

I eye the balloon that is now collapsed on the ground. Its envelope burns as the wind fans the flames. I count eight bodies scattered on the ground. Emergency crew workers work frantically to contain the horror that burns into my retinas. Fire hoses spew gallons of water onto the field. The thumping of helicopters circling above.

"He's over here!" the firefighter shouts as we draw near to where the victim is located.

"What's his condition?" I yell back.

"Critical. I'd say about ninety percent of his body is pretty well toasted."

"Yikes."

I smell it – the acrid odor of burnt human flesh.

"Did anyone get his name?" asks Trevor.

"Someone went through his wallet looking for a way to contact a relative. Said his name is Ronald something. Can't remember the last name."

The firefighter steps aside.

I leave Trevor with the equipment. Approach the victim.

I stare with dumb terror at the spectacle that lies on the blue tarp that's spread over the ground.

"Anything else?" the firefighter asks.

I lift a glance. "Naw. We're good."

"Thanks, guy."

"You bet."

The firefighter hurries away.

The din of chaos rattles my senses. The thumping of the rotor blades pounds at my ears.

I throw my airbag to the ground. Drop to my knees. Examine Ron's face. I eye the heavily charred flesh, speckled with bits of pink underscoring the charred skin that curls upward – like he'd been shaved by a cheap potato peeler. Fragments of burned clothing peer out from under blackened tissue.

Looks like he's been roasted over an open fire pit.

I wanted to say it. I didn't dare.

"Hi Ron," I say with a soothing tone.

I look deep into his eyes.

"How are you doing?"

His mouth opens. Eyes teem with crushing pain. He breathes out a barely audible whisper, "It hurts." He winces. "It hurts really bad."

I glance at Trevor. He's busily preparing for treatment. I lift Ron's hand gently. I place it into mine. "I'm going to do everything I can to make this better for you," I say softly. "We're going to get you to the hospital as quickly as we can. The best thing you can do is to remain as calm as possible. I know you're in a lot of pain, but if you can just stay calm and allow us to do our work, it will be easier for you all the way around."

Ron takes hold of my arm. Pulls me toward him. I shudder with the terror that emanates from his gaze.

"I'm going to die, aren't I?"

A salient void fills the gap between us.

"We're going to do everything we can to make sure that doesn't happen," I say.

An unexpected gust of wind deposits a fresh scent of burnt flesh into my mouth, causing a strong desire to vomit.

Ron releases his grip.

The question settles in my brain.

I already know the likelihood of surviving a ninety percent burn is less than one percent. We all know it. And he's not displaying any evidence of beating those odds.

But who am I to say whether he lives or dies? I'm not God.

I clock a glance around then back to Ron.

His face constricts with pain. I push back the desire to cry.

Why do people have to suffer like this? Why?

I continue to assess the patient's condition – wondering where do I start? How do I touch him? How do I not add to his suffering?

Trevor works hurriedly to assemble the oxygen

equipment, prepare the contents for the IV, and remove the basic life support material needed to ensure a smooth and seamless treatment for the patient.

"Trevor, hand me the penlight, would ya?"

Trevor reaches into the bag. Hands me the penlight.

I peer into Ron's eyes. His eyelashes have been completely burned off. So has the hair in his nostrils.

He must have inhaled the flames.

The image of his larynx, esophagus, and lungs burning inside sends a chill up my spine.

I flash a ray of light into the pupil to assess the level of dilation. *Not good.*

"His eyes aren't responding," I say. "Let's get an IV started in the cephalic vein in the antecubital fossa area."

Trevor hurries to start the IV at the bend in Ron's right arm where the antecubital fossa is located. The thick cephalic vein makes an entry for the catheter so much easier.

I place my fingers on the radial artery located in his right wrist while I continue to monitor the condition of his body.

His pulse is quickening.

I lift the left wrist to prepare for the other IV. There's a presidential Rolex cloaked in soot planted securely on the area where we need to insert the needle.

"I need to remove your watch."

"No," Ron replies.

"I'm a watch collector. I own one of these. I know how to remove it." He nods approval. I remove the watch. "I'll make sure it gets to your family."

"Let's get him ready for a c-spine mobilization," I add.

"Are we going to intubate?" asks Trevor.

"Probably. Let me have the stethoscope."

I insert the earpiece while Trevor prepares the oxygen tank for intubation. I place the chest piece lightly on the patient. His heart rate has increased and his breathing is erratic. The light in his eyes fades and a dim film appears.

"What am I going to tell my wife?" Ron asks with a tone of resignation.

"I'll take care of that for you," I say pensively.

The thumping helicopters cant into view circling for a place to land. I quickly pull the tarp over the three of us to avoid airborne particles landing on Ron's skin. The foul odor of burned flesh is now contained, intensifying, filling my lungs, causing every cell in my body to retch at the acrid burnt offering.

"I've got so much to do," Ron cries suddenly with a raspy voice. "I can't die now. I've got too much to do."

His words hit me, and I wonder what I would do if that were me, lying there, knowing I only had minutes to live. I shake the thought away.

"My wife." He strains to breathe. "I can't leave her with all that responsibility."

"I know it's hard, but you've got to remain calm. Let's focus on you, right now, okay?"

I continue checking vitals.

"We had such good times together," Ron struggles with short rapid breaths, his speech truncating into short incomplete sentences.

"Really good times."

He exhales a breath.

"We made...

Beautiful babies together.

Grew a business together."

He grunts.

"Lived life well,

together."

"Yeah?" I meet his gaze with a quick glance of admiration. "What kind of business do you have?"

"We own a plant in the Atlanta area."

He takes a moment.

"We worked so hard to get that business.

Mortgaged our house.

We worked ten, twelve, eighteen hours a day."

He winces.

"It was our greatest accomplishment."

"Oh. So you don't live here?" I ask.

"No." His voice is gravelly, weak. "Visiting from Atlanta...

Thought it would be fun," his face scrunches.

"To take a hot air balloon ride."

A chasm of silence.

"Tell her I love her, would you?"

The request deposits itself in the middle of my chest.

"Tell her I love her."

"Tell her…" His voice trembles. He blinks away tears. "She is the only woman I have ever loved."

He pauses to gain his composure.

"Would you do that for me?" he adds.

"Absolutely."

I avoid his gaze. I know I will never see his wife. I feel guilty lying to him. I justify it by assessing what really matters – and what really matters is easing his pain. This time, it's the emotional pain. That's all.

The helicopters land. Three EMTs run toward us carrying a large yellow board that looks like an oversized ironing board with holes in it.

I turn my attention to Ron. I have to yell so he can hear me. Rotor blades throwing gusts of wind make it difficult to communicate. "We're going to place you on a board and stabilize your body just in case there may be some spinal injuries."

I hold onto his hand, comforting him until the EMTs arrive. One EMT stabilizes Ron's head while another secures his neck with a C collar.

The EMTs work in sync, steadying Ron so they can roll him on his side, place the backboard underneath him, and lower him onto the board.

Ron cries out as they work. They carefully anchor him with a spider strap – a long horizontal orange strap with five black perpendicular appendages resembling a spider – to ensure there is no movement during transport. I place foam blocks on each side of his head, taping the forehead and chin to the board while Trevor ties his hands together with gauze.

The film in Ron's eyes thickens to a milky glaze. I fight back the natural tendency to weep.

Why do such good people have to die such tragic deaths?

The questions keep coming.

I have no answer.

I lift a glance to Trevor. "Let's get him intubated."

Trevor pulls an oral airway from the bag, and places it between Ron's teeth. He inserts the tube into Ron's mouth, then guides the tubing into Ron's lungs while I work on the flow of oxygen.

I hand the oxygen tank to Trevor.

I lift Ron's hand into mine while two other EMTs hoist the backboard into the air. Trevor carries the oxygen tank. All four of us run the backboard to the helicopter that will air lift Ron to the nearest hospital.

The wind whips as the doors close. Ron is on his way to the hospital and will more than likely expire by the time he arrives. There's nothing more we can do. Our job is done.

It all seems so futile.

We head back to the blue tarp to clean up. Thoughts of what had just transpired swirl in my brain. I reflect on the mom and the drowning child, the watering down of my boots, my sister, the girl with the bare chest.

And my own behavior. I can be rude, crude, and as crass as the best of them. And what does that get me? More of the same.

"I'll gather the garbage, Trevor. You wanna get the equipment?"

"Sure."

I gather unused supplies and place them in the airbag.

I think of life and how we suffer, not just how we suffer, but how we contribute to each other's suffering, just by mere comments made or jokes played.

I locate an empty garbage bag.

I'm getting tired of it. Tired of the trauma of life.

I exhale a heavy breath.

I want to do something about it. But what? What can I do?

We work in silence. I continue to ponder the complexities of my questions – my thoughts.

Maybe I want to understand more about life – about people. But what does that mean?

I pause as I think more about the answer to that question.

I don't know. Maybe there is no answer.
I continue cleaning – thinking.
How can we become a better populace?
That's the question.
I roll the tarp. Secure the trash bag. We head to the ambulance.
It's time to see Mary.

SEVEN

February 6, 1989 – 4:17 PM

I unlatch the gate to the white picket fence. Close the gate behind me.

Strolling down the walkway toward the blue-gray house, I can't help but notice how immaculate Mary's yard is – lush green grass perfectly trimmed with flowerbeds strategically placed around its circumference. A huge oak tree stands in the middle of the yard to the left of the walkway and is designed to provide much needed shade from the summertime sun. I pull on the screen that shields the entryway and knock on the red door with a southern exposure.

Thoughts of Mary pervade my mind. It's been seven weeks since I made my decision to see her. Not sure what took me so long. Fear, I guess. Fear of what she might say. Fear of reliving that deep connection.

The door opens. She meets my gaze.

"Hey, Jimmy." She places her arms around my neck giving me a gentle hug.

Streaks of golden highlights glimmer through dark brown hair. A hair clip holds the style in place.

She releases her hold and steps back to give me the once over.

Glancing back, I make my own observations.

"You're looking good, Jimmy."

She's beautiful for a woman her age. Slender body. Dressed in black yoga pants with a matching tee shirt. Mid-fifties I'd guess.

"What have you been doing with yourself these days?"

I hesitate, then peer into dark brown eyes.

"Nothin'," I reply.

"Well, c'mon in. Can I get you something to drink? Coffee? Water?"

"Water's fine."

"Have a seat. I'll be right back."

I scan the room for a place to sit. The simplicity of Mary's decor and the way she uses color to bring out the excellence in every piece is striking to me. I take a seat in one of the two candy apple red club chairs that face the sofa of the same color. Wooden floors showcase an exquisitely crafted area rug highlighting dark walnut accent tables to add a rustic touch. The walls are painted the color of straw and are accented with the just the right amount of wall decor to pull the finishing touch together. It's shaded and cool inside. Not anything like the firehouse where it can be bright and hot most of the time, save for the air conditioning.

Mary enters the room.

"Here ya go, Jimmy."

"You look comfortable in that outfit," I say.

"You're used to seeing me in my nurse's uniform, aren't you?"

"Yeah," I smile. "You look good."

"Thanks." She hands me a bottle of water, plops herself onto the sofa, brings her feet up. We chat a few minutes. My body relaxes. My fear subsides.

I like Mary. She's easy to talk to once I get past my fears. She has a depth about her that is attractive to me. And I love the way she carries herself, simple, yet confident, with a posture about her that is firm and strong.

She takes a sip of water.

I lean forward mating my fingers.

"Look, Mary. If you don't mind, I'm just going to cut right to the chase."

"Yeah. Sure. What's going on?"

I exhale a long stream of air.

"I've been thinking about life... about people."

"What about them?"

"Well..." I rub my chin. "There's a couple of calls I've gone on that kind of shook me up."

"How so, Jimmy?"

"You know how we treat people sometimes."

"I've heard rumors," Mary says.

"Like?"

"Like, I've heard how some of you guys handle your patients like they're nothing more than a bag of groceries – load 'em up in the ambulance, drop 'em off at the hospital. Business as usual. No heart. No mercy. That sort of thing."

"Yeah. Well, there's more." I purse my lips. "Some of us are downright cruel to our patients. We're known to make snide remarks and even let the patient know what an inconvenience they are to us. We pay no mind to the suffering they might be going through. Not everybody does it, and not all the time, but enough. I can be just as guilty as the rest."

"I see a lot of you guys taking some of those calls pretty hard," Mary says as she reaches for her bottle of water.

"True. But that's beside the point. I'm talking about calls where we act as if we're the only ones that matter."

I take a breath.

"I've been on a few calls lately, where I've been seeing... no... *feeling* the patient's pain. *Feeling* their suffering. And it's just got me thinking."

"Thinking about what?"

"About people. About life. How we hurt. How we cause each other's suffering."

I clear my throat.

"So, I'm thinking I want to make a difference,

maybe treat people better. Make their life experience happier. You know, stop the suffering."

"I see." Mary casts a gaze to the floor.

"That's why I'm here. I know you know a lot about life. I've heard your comments. We've talked. I know you know stuff."

"I know too much," Mary says.

"Too much?"

She exhales a heavy sigh while lowering her legs to draw closer. With sincere expression, she catches my eye. A shiver of warmth surges through me. I blink. Close my eyes. Shut it down.

"Jimmy. You're so young. What are ya? Twenty-two? Twenty-three?"

"Twenty-four." I say as I lift a guarded gaze.

"Twenty-four." Mary shakes her head. "I look into those hazel green eyes behind wire rimmed glasses, and I see such a gentle and kind soul in that handsome round face. That's one of the many qualities I like about you, Jimmy. You have such a caring spirit."

"Maybe. When I'm not contributing to the problem."

"Oh, stop. I know you do way more to help people than you do to contribute to their problem."

Mary leans back into the sofa.

"You can't stop the suffering, Jimmy. It's an integral part of life. And you can't make people happier. That is up to them."

Mary pauses. Pins my gaze.

"What?" I say.

"So, why don't you just start treating people better? I mean, why are you *really* here – when all you have to do is simply stop behaving in a hurtful manner?"

"Because sometimes I can't control my reaction. It's like an automatic response."

I pull my eyeglasses. Rub my eyes.

"I want to do more than just treat people better, Mary. I want to set the standard. I want to be the example others can follow, and I don't know how to do that. I don't know that I know enough about people to do what I want to do, and I don't know what I don't know, and that is why I am here."

A long pause. Mary looks fixedly into my eyes. I feel my expression soften.

"We've talked, Mary. I know you know stuff," I repeat.

I hold her gaze expectantly. She clocks a glance around the living room that is growing darker by the minute, and I can tell Mary is hesitant to share.

"What's holding you back, Mary?"

She leans to turn on a lamp.

"Jimmy, people don't care about this stuff. Whenever I talk about it, their eyes glaze over, and suddenly I'm feeling like a martian."

"What's that got to do with me?"

"Oh, I don't know. Thinking you'll probably do the same."

"Try me."

Mary probes my gaze.

I let her.

She adjusts her tee shirt. Looks me in the eye. Resigns herself to a "Fine. But if I see any evidence that you're losing interest, I'll stop and I won't go on. Got it?"

"I'm good with that."

"Okay," she purses her lips. "Someone gave me a book a long time ago. Told me to read it. It was the vehicle that started me on the journey of discovery that I'm about to share with you, now."

I shrug indifference, not really caring about the details, and praying to God she's not going to suggest I read a stupid book.

I note the change in her expression. It reflects my thought. "Okay, Jimmy. I'll get to the point."

"Thanks, Mary."

She shifts her position. A serious stare pins my gaze. She begins.

"Now, if you can understand that we are really nothing more than an energetic vibrational communication system, looking to align with like kind vibrations, then you will understand people and life in a way that most people can't even begin to comprehend," Mary says.

I feel myself giving her a blank stare. I catch her eyeing me. She's already lost me.

"I promise you, I'll try. If it will help me to accomplish what I want to accomplish, I will try," I say.

"Very good." She takes a sip of water. "Then let's begin."

Mary talks of the point of conception, how we're a blank slate of energy soaking in information like a sponge that soaks in water.

"Our sponge, (Mary traces quote marks in the air) starts to fill the moment we are conceived, and it is through our feeling self that we receive information. At this stage of life, and for a long time to come, all information that is fed to us is through energy and its vibration."

I question her, wanting to get a deeper understanding of what she is trying to convey.

"Well, you gotta know I'm not a scientist by any stretch of the imagination and I don't know the jargon, but I'll do my best to break it down."

"Fair enough."

She tells me that all living things communicate, kind of like radio waves, how the process begins at inception and continues through gestation, and how these radio waves vibrate at different frequencies. How we're infused with them. Can't make cognitive decisions about them. We simply receive the information. Soak it up, whether it serves us or not. How we get to deal with the effects throughout our lives.

"And we have no clue that there are a bunch of these little boogers driving our life circumstances and running our emotions," Mary says.

I push my eyeglasses to the bridge of my nose.

"Silent communications."

"Hey. I like that," Mary says. "That's exactly what I'm talking about."

I smile.

"While in utero and for the first few years of life, our communication systems (Mary patterns the air with another set of quotes) are building with these radio waves, all vibrating at different frequencies. We don't have the ability to judge or make cognitive decisions about what we're receiving. We simply receive because we can't stop the inflow from becoming one with our being, and *WE* get to deal with the effect of that throughout our whole lives – good and bad." Mary huffs a snort. "Best part about it is we don't even know it's going on." She exhales a heavy sigh. "We have no clue these pesky little critters are driving our life circumstances and running our emotions."

I rub my chin. "How do we get exposed to these radio waves, Mary? I mean because we're inside the womb, right? Where we're protected?"

"Well, you'd think so, wouldn't you?" Mary says. "Actually, while in the womb, most of the vibrational elements come from mom, through food, drink, and her emotional state. Whether she drinks alcohol, smokes cigarettes, or even eats healthy – it all affects the baby during gestation and deposits experiences in the form of vibrational energy into the baby's being."

"So, that's why everybody dotes over moms

telling them what to do and what not to do."

"Yes. Because everything that affects the mother's body, both inside and out, affects the unborn child. And if I remember right, early in his discovery, Dr. Janov was linking a host of neuroses, illnesses, homosexuality, and other abnormal behaviors to life in the womb and to birthing experiences."

"Homosexuality?" An image of my brother flashes to mind.

"Yeah."

Mary continues to talk about the messaging system, how it builds through womb life, through the birthing process, throughout childhood, and how it drives our adult lives.

My mind wanders back to the time my brother had to tell my parents he had AIDS.

I remember how awful it was, my father glaring at him with the question of "how could you be so stupid?" planted squarely onto his face. My mother going ape-shit over the news, yelling, "You're going to die. You're going to die," followed with, "we can beat this. You'll see. We'll beat this. I love you. I don't want you to die." The tone of her voice all co-dependent sounding. I felt as if my brother was being verbally pummeled. It seemed to me that my father cared more about the fact his son was gay than he did about the fact that my brother had a deadly disease. I remember how my brother handled it. Not well. I could see it on his face. It made me want to cry for him. I wanted to help him, but I couldn't. I was just a kid – a thirteen-year-old helpless kid.

"My brother's gay," I say.

"Yeah?"

"You think his homosexuality comes from something in the womb?"

"I have no idea, Jimmy. Could be. Could be from birthing. I think it's a subject matter that's still being worked on."

"I see."

Mary prattles on about the difference between a child who is loved and wanted versus the child who is demeaned, the child who is never touched, the child who never hears the words, "I love you," and how they generate different lives. One of success and wealth. One of drugs and promiscuity. She tells of Dr. Janov, the psychiatrist who discovered Primal Scream Therapy, how he takes the patient back in time to as far back as womb life to relieve the patient of the neuroses, the illnesses, the neurotic emotional states of being that he or she suffers, and how I should do the therapy.

"Do the therapy?" I say with a startle.

"Yeah. You should do the therapy."

"Y-e-e-a-a-h... I don't think so, Mary. It's not something I'm really ready to do."

"Well, you should."

The comment delivers an uncomfortable moment of silence.

"So what you are saying, Mary, is that all that the baby just went through will create its life?"

"It will be the fundamental building blocks to drive it in a general direction, yes, but let me clarify something here. Vibrational communication systems communicate through energy and not necessarily through the specific meaning or execution of a word or series of words. It is the vibration of the words, the energy of the words that are at play. We humans are trained to operate from the brain, and so we define things with more concrete concepts such as words. Vibrational systems operate from the feeling part of who we are. And so vibrations can pull together situations that might otherwise be divided by words."

"A little tough to grasp, you know, because of the world we live in," I say.

"I understand. But I'm talking about the world we *really* live in. The one we *can't* see."

"Right," I say tenuously – struggling to absorb the information.

"We are so vast and so deep in our vibrational structure that it is hard to tell what vibrations will have the strongest power or how they will align with each other to create an event. I mean you just can't state a specific here. It's impossible. The only thing you can do is gain an understanding of the flow, enough to make general statements of probabilities and enough to understand why one might behave irrationally or respond in a manner the way they do."

I pinch my chin. I feel a question rise in my expression.

"Mary, all this new information is a little hard to grasp. Maybe it will help if you can tell me how I can use this information to help me to become the example others can follow?"

I catch a look of "how do I explain this?" cross her expression as she waits a beat.

"If you can understand the fundamental concepts of how life operates, then you will know that the things that trigger you are about something inside of you that you aren't aware of, and you can use that information to step away from the situation, not make it about you and behave in a manner such that you no longer are a participant in the problem but a vehicle for a solution."

I blink my eyes, not fully comprehending the message in her words. "Yeah. Okay, Mary. What's a trigger?"

"A trigger is an event that causes an automatic negative response – usually one of anger or sorrow. The trigger can be anything, like a song that causes sadness or spoken words that make us angry. There's a natural tendency for us to defend our pain, hence the reactions we sometimes can't control."

"Ah," I say as I lift a forefinger to my temple, making a connection I can finally understand.

"I have found that when I separate myself from

the drama someone else is trying to engage me in, when I don't have any emotional purchase in the situation, that the one who is triggered falls in line with me. That person becomes calmer. Tension eases and the life experience has improved, even if only for that moment," Mary adds.

"Really," I say with intrigue.

"Yup. But I have removed the vibration inside of me. It doesn't percolate there anymore. That is the difference."

"Can I remove my vibrations?"

"If you do the therapy."

"I'm not ready for that," I say.

"Then, you'll just have to work at it a little harder. That's all."

Mary rises. "Jimmy. I got the midnight shift tonight."

"Oh. I'm sorry, Mary. I didn't realize..."

"Not to worry, Jimmy. I didn't tell you." She smiles. "C'mon. I'll walk you to the door."

Mary opens the door. I step outside, turn to thank her while the conversation, bubbling like a cesspool, churns in my mind.

"Hey, Jimmy. When's the last time you visited your parents?"

I pause a moment while I ponder the question. "Gee. I don't know. Why do you ask?"

"You should visit your parents, Jimmy."

"Why?"

"They're family. There's nothing like nurturing

the family relationships. It's the fabric of life."

"I guess," I let a tense moment linger.

Mary leans against the door jam. "Listen, Jim. I know we covered quite a bit. If you have any questions or need clarity, stop by, okay?"

"I'll take you up on that," I smile, step away. Mary starts to retreat behind the door when she stops to yell, "And go see your parents!"

Half way down the walkway, I turn, give her a mock salute, check my watch, and walk to my car.

EIGHT

February 6, 1989 – 6:29 PM

I approach the door to my parent's home. It's slightly ajar. I push gently, step into the living room.

"Ma?" I call out.

Glowing lamps shed light into the stillness. A quick glance around reveals the same old sofa. The same old recliner. The same old end tables. The same old wingback chairs. Every item in the room is some form of a drab shade of brown. The furniture is systematically arranged along walls painted in the ever-popular shade of Navajo white. The décor is dated, but the place is clean and well-maintained. I'm proud to call it home.

"Ma?" I call out again as I walk the berber carpet past the fireplace.

"In here, Jimmy." a gruff voice responds.

I follow the sound into the kitchen and my senses immediately fill with the scent of cooked food. "Mmm. Somethin' smells good."

Mom mumbles something I don't quite catch.

I nod at my dad who's sitting at the square oak table located just to the right of the entry way. I swear that table's been in the family a hundred years.

"Hey, Jimmy. What brings you around?" Dad says.

"Oh. Just thought I'd drop by. That's all," I reply as I scan the familiar surroundings.

Nothing has changed. The same white curtains with ruffled edges that border the tiered design still drape the windows. Ivory appliances peer out from dark wood-stained cabinets. Formica countertops of the same color are cluttered with cookware, spices, and other helpful tools. Yellow and gold-veined vinyl flooring add a pop of color. Plenty of light beams from the kitchen soffit. A smattering of artwork adorns the walls.

I glance at my mother. She's working in the horseshoe-shaped kitchen, hovering over a pot of something that's cooking stovetop. She collects two pot holders, lifts a heavy pot, and carries it to the sink. I saunter over to the stove, peer into the pot she leaves behind. "Watcha cookin'?"

"Your favorite, Jimmy," she says. "Spaghetti."

Spittles of red pop out of the pot and onto the

surface. I inhale the rising steam, then naturally pick up a utensil to taste.

"Oh, no you don't, Jimmy. Grab a spoon outta the drawer." Ma says as she drains the contents into the colander. "And no double dipping!"

I take the spoon out of the drawer, dip into the pot. "Mmmm." I smack my lips. "I swear you make the best spaghetti sauce on the planet," I say.

"It's the Italian in me," Mom says.

"Oh, get out!" I snort a laugh. "You ain't got any Italian in you."

"You wouldn't know it by the spaghetti sauce now, woudja?"

I walk over to the sink, place the spoon in the well.

She's a small-statured woman. Strands of gray peek out of sandy blonde hair. It's shoulder length. She's got the sides wrapped behind her ears. Her light brown eyes peer through red-rimmed eye glasses. She's wearing an apron over Mary Tyler Moore slacks and a white button-down blouse. She grins as she wipes the sweat from her forehead with the front of her forearm.

"I guess you're right, Ma." I give her a peck on the cheek.

"I know I'm right," she smiles. "But don't tell anybody. It's our secret." She winks.

"You're crazy, Martha," my dad says. He smirks at me. "Your mother's a nut."

I shake my head. Take a seat at the table.

Dribs and drabs of Mary's conversation dart in and out of my mind as does the veil of my unnatural connection to her. The thing about the vibration of the words seem to be sticking hardest. I'm thinking I'm going to have Mary explain that to me.

"Wanna beer?" my father asks.

"Sure," I say.

He opens the fridge, pulls two bottles of beer, pops the caps. "How's work?"

I gulp a swallow. "Oh. You know. Same shit. Different day."

"Nothing's changed?" he asks.

"No. If anything, it's getting worse."

"Son..." He drops the comment. Shakes his head.

I reflect on the many conversations my dad and I have had on this subject. The shitty furniture. Appliances that don't work. The equipment they make us work with – old and dated. They spend more money on repairs than if they'd just break down and buy new stuff. But management won't do it. "Costs too much," they say. Sometimes I wonder how we manage to do our jobs. And don't let me get started on the pay. We're so underpaid for what we do... like the security guards who monitor gated communities. I take a swig of beer. "Yeah...nothing like getting paid the same wage as a security guard...like they're responsible for life and death checking cars at a gate."

Dad leans into the table. "Son..."

"And the way management treats us? It's unconscionable. They play favorites. Mess with our schedules. Like it's a real honor to be working in such substandard conditions while getting paid minimum wage."

"I'm tellin' ya..." Dad says.

"Did I tell you about Frank?" I ask.

"Nu-uh. What happened?" I eye Dad's meaty hand as he lifts the bottle of beer.

"He just finished a call and was on his way to the station. He was stopped at a red light. Like a complete stop. You know, foot on the brake, waiting for the light to turn green. And someone rear ends the ambulance, pushes it into the intersection, and the ambulance collides with another vehicle."

"Oh. Wow. Was he hurt?" my dad asks.

"No, but the company blamed Frank for the accident. Said he caused it."

"You're kidding," my father says with an arched eyebrow.

Mother fuckers.

I take a swallow of beer.

"Nope. And they stripped him of his driving privileges, too," I add.

"I'm not surprised," Dad says. "You've said in the past that it's standard practice – to strip them of their driving privileges when they get into an accident regardless of whose fault it is."

"I know, but it doesn't make it right," I say. "They cut your pay when you can't drive. And

Frank's got two little ones at home and a wife who doesn't work."

"That's a shame," my dad says. He runs his fingers through his thinning brown hair. "I'm telling you, Jimmy. You need to get a union in there."

"You know I don't like 'em, Dad."

"It'd stop shit like that from happening," he says.

I love my dad. He's a handsome man. Would love to think I take after him, but I don't. Well, maybe some. He's of average height. Has hazel eyes. Round face. Muscular, but with a small paunch.

My dad's a strong union guy, too. Works hard for the organization. Believes in the concept. Loves what the brotherhood does for him. He knows people in high places. Runs the local chapter at the fire station where he works.

"So, your union still treating you good?" I ask.

"Of course," he says as if it's a foregone conclusion.

"I think you should get married, Jimmy." Ma places three large plates on the table. "Get a decent job. Make me some grandbabies."

"Oh, Ma. Is that all you ever think about?"

"Well, your brother is never going to give me a grandchild and your sister... well... I know she has Jacob, but he's nearly an adult, and it doesn't look like Carol's interested in having more."

"Isn't one enough?" I ask.

"I want more," Mom says. "I want babies." She places forks and knives alongside the plates.

"I'm just not ready for that yet, Ma. Besides, I like what I do."

I eye the place setting. Think of Mary. Wonder if my mother really is responsible for my brother being gay.

"Have you heard from either Robbie or Carol?" I ask.

Robbie's my brother. Carol's my sister.

"We don't hear from Robbie, much," Dad says.

"I spoke with Carol just last week," says Mom.

"Yeah? How's she doing?"

"Well, she loves her son, that's for sure."

Mom sets a serving dish of spaghetti noodles tabletop.

"I wish she'd find him a daddy. Make me some grandbabies."

"Oh, Ma."

"You wanna nudder beer, Jimmy?" Dad asks.

"Naw. I gotta drive."

"You workin' tomorrow?"

"Nope." I place my hands on the table as if to ready myself to depart. "Got the day off."

"Then why don't you stay the night."

I stop. Eye him hesitantly.

"Dad. I really can't."

"Sure you can. We still have your bed and you can have supper with us." Dad takes another two bottles of beer from the fridge. Mom delivers a bowl of spaghetti sauce. "Have dinner with us, Jimmy," Mom implores.

"We can play Backgammon and drink beer till the cows come home," Dad adds. "Come on. It'll be fun. Besides, your mom makes the best spaghetti in the world. You said so yourself."

"Stay, Jimmy," Mom says. "We don't get to see you much anymore."

I read the plea in their eyes. Get that sinking feeling.

Fuck.

I exhale a heavy sigh. "You know I play a mean game of Backgammon, don'tcha?"

My mom serves the spaghetti.

"We'll see," Dad says as he lifts a helping from his plate.

"Mm hmm. Yes, we will, Dad, cuz I'm gonna whoop your butt," I chuckle.

"Uh huh. That depends on how much beer I can get you to drink." Dad smiles.

NINE

I follow Mary into the kitchen. She flips a switch. A light beams.

"How about a ham and cheese?" she asks as she approaches the black refrigerator that is nestled tightly between two lightly veined granite countertops. I take a seat at the round oak table centered in the room. Glance at the light brown contemporary cabinets mounted on reddish orange walls – the floor tiled in cream, the window framed with yellow curtains patterned in colorful flowers. I eye the darkness of night that blankets the back yard.

"Sure," I say as I take a seat. I exhale an audible sigh.

"What's up, Jimmy? Is this getting to be too much for you?"

"No. I was just thinking."

"Thinking about what?"

"Thinking about what you said when you talked about the vibration of the word, how it speaks a different language than we do."

"Yeah? What about it?"

"I was hoping maybe you could talk about that a little more."

"Sure."

Mary drifts to the table and delivers two red plates topped with ham and cheese sandwiches, potato chips on the side. She takes a seat. I scoot the plate closer to me and take hold of the sandwich.

"When I bring up the word *anger,* what comes to mind?" She takes a bite of her sandwich.

"I don't know." I cast a gaze toward the ceiling. "People who are mad at each other? People who fight, argue?"

"I think that's how most people see anger. But what if I told you that energy of anger expands beyond what we've been programmed to see."

"What do you mean?"

"I think I can illustrate best with an example," Mary says as she pulls her plate closer. She lifts a potato chip.

"I know someone – let's call her Jane – who is your ordinary everyday average person. The kind of person who is respectful and rarely raises her voice. I've never seen her display behavior that indicates she has anger issues. She's always very nice, obedient, generous, raised by parents who were old school. Jane avoids confrontation...."

My mind drifts with thoughts of Mary – previous encounters – as Mary continues to speak about Jane. The Jane who reads motivational books to become a better person. The Jane who practices and implements what she reads. The Jane who has issues – the biggest one being money.

"Then one day Jane reads a book that tells her how she can have whatever she wants in life. All she has to do is ask the Universe for the thing she desires, and the Universe will put into motion the things needed to send it her way. She just has to have faith. Believe."

Mary catches my attention.

"So Jane's doing whatever she does to ask the Universe for money, right? And then one day she telephones to tell me she's been in a car accident. Someone rear-ended her, and I can feel her counting the money she thinks she's going to get. And she gets it, but it's not the amount she was thinking."

"How much did she get?" I say.

"Like fifteen hundred dollars," Mary says. "Way less than what she was expecting."

"Anyway," Mary bites into her sandwich. "She continues asking the Universe for money. And a month or so later, she's rear-ended by a city street sweeper. Aside from being bummed out, she's a bit concerned that she's been in two car accidents so close together and neither of them her fault. Just kind of strikes her as a bit odd, the request for money and the accidents, the timing and all. She makes note of it but moves on, chalking it up to life."

"Crap like that happens to people, ya know." I take another bite of sandwich.

"I know," Mary says.

I eye Mary. Wonder why I'm so sensitive to her. Why that connection runs deep.

"It's the vibration of anger," Mary adds.

I arch an eyebrow.

Hmmm. The vibration of anger. I chuckle to myself, as if that were the answer to my question.

"But that's beside the point," Mary continues. "Things like that don't happen to Jane, so she shrugs it off, thinking it's just coincidence. And she did get paid money, even though it was a smaller amount than she thought she should have been paid. I mean, after all, it was a city vehicle that hit her."

It was common knowledge growing up, that if you were to get into an accident, you do it with a city vehicle, because you always got paid better when the city was involved. Either things have changed or it simply isn't true.

"Turns out she got paid the same amount as the first accident, about fifteen hundred dollars," Mary says.

"You're kidding."

"Huh uh." Mary snorts a chuckle. "But, she's determined to make this work so she continues to ask for money. Several weeks later she is rear-ended again, but this time she's really questioning the coincidence."

"How so?" I say to Mary.

"She realizes the accidents started when she asked the Universe for money. I mean, she's been in accidents before, but not like this, not so close together, and not so many, and none of them her fault. She wonders what's wrong. She can't understand why the Universe is doing this. So she quits asking for money. And guess what?"

"What?"

"The accidents stop."

"No shit." I lift a potato chip through a moment of silence. "So, what you're saying, Mary is that the Universe gave her what she asked for but not the way she wanted to receive it?"

"No, Jimmy. I'm saying that the Universe revealed her internal vibration of anger by bringing what she asked for through an angry vehicle, no pun intended," Mary smiles. "Even though she showed no outward signs of anger, it was clearly resonating at some level within her body, and I'll bet money that if she did the internal work that I did, she'd find a ton of it."

I probe her face questioningly. "But Mary,

couldn't you say it was coincidence?"

"You could. Maybe it was. But the point here is the energy in which the money shows up. So, maybe the reason it was car accidents this time is because that's what was available to the Universe in that given timeframe."

"I'm not so sure I buy into that," I say.

"Would it have made any difference if it showed up through say... an ugly legal battle?"

I think on that. "Hmm. I guess not."

"Precisely."

I finger the potato chips as I work to wrap my mind around the concept. I catch Mary eyeing me while I'm engaged in thought.

"I remember a time when my life was beleaguered with mean and ugly people. Hurtful people. Hurtful situations. It seemed to be a way of life to consistently attract this kind of aggressive, contemptible behavior," Mary continues.

I gaze at her fixedly, thinking of how unusual my sensitivity is to her. The depth of the connection. The seeming extraterrestrial feel to it.

She prattles on about her lack of understanding, her confusion over the unrelenting stream of nasties that seemed to show up in her life, the unanswered questions. While she talks about her personal journey of self-discovery, I marvel at how I can feel her thoughts. Hear her mind.

"Early on, before I decided to become a nurse, I had taken a job with a local law firm, and I remember my boss being a class one Type A bitch with a capital B – a rare form of nasty. Didn't think they made 'em that bad." Mary shakes her head.

One could almost interpret it as romantic. Could be, but it's not. She's old enough to be my mother, and I'm just not that guy.

"One day something happened, and I can't remember what it was, but she unloaded her nasty shit on me, and instead of feeding into her denigrating rhetoric, I did something that was really hard to do. I took it, and while I was biting my tongue, I asked myself one question, "What is inside of me that brought this kind of person to me?"

I struggle with keeping the friendship on level ground, but sometimes it's hard to do. When you know someone that intimately. When you know what they're going to say. When you can hear their thoughts.

"I worked on that question for several weeks, and what I discovered was abhorrent. Inside of me was mountains of anger, comingled with evil, cowardice, hatred, vile stuff, stuff that felt like the devil. It was horrifying." Mary shivers.

Sometimes, I feel like Mary has pirated my inner world.

"I couldn't believe what I was feeling way down deep inside of me, the ugliness of it, the putrid stuff that came from my father. I managed to purge that sewage from inside of me and replace it with a truth that I wanted to own. And you wanna know what happened?"

"What?"

"Almost immediately people started treating me differently, and angry people and angry experiences quit showing up in my life. I wasn't looking for a result, but the change was so blatant, I would have had to have been dead not to notice it."

I ponder her words as I resign myself to accept the fact that I guess I will never know, why the sensitivity, why the deep connection, why her.

"There was no denying it. My boss never uttered an angry word to me again. She was consistently respectful and remained that way until I left the firm," Mary adds.

We bite into our sandwiches, her words spinning in my head.

"Do you know that to this day I still do not attract mean and nasty people?" she continues.

"Really," I state disbelievingly.

"Honest to God."

I mull over her story.

"You have to feel this shit, Jimmy. And that takes a process."

"The Dr. Janov thing?"

"Yup."

I think on the conversation.

"What about trauma victims, Mary? How does this play out with trauma victims?"

"I don't really know for sure, but I'm going to go

out on a limb here and say that I believe it is all based on the same principles that I have been discussing with you."

"Explain."

"It makes sense to me," Mary says. "Plus, I have my own experience that I draw from. If we are truly a vibrating universe that is in constant communication, then we must be attracting trauma situations as well."

"That's a hard buy," I state.

"I know. But people's decisions and desires are driven by something, and it has to be the vibrational pattern within them. Think about this, Jimmy. Think about two people of the same physical and mental capabilities who engage in a life-threatening situation. They both have equal opportunity to escape, and both have strong desire to do so, but only one does. Why is that? Can you come up with a viable explanation?"

"It could be any number of reasons," I say.

"Yeah. Just like any number of vibrational patterns that are communicating to you on a subterranean level, if you get my drift. I think it is the vibrational communication system deep within us that will put us in situations of trauma because we are unknowingly asking for it."

"Asking for it?" I shake my head. "That's rough."

"I know. Consciously, it's tough to put a mind around. I have a hard time with it myself, but that's my conclusion, and I have no proof or evidence to support the theory other than my own research and personal life experiences."

Mary narrows her eyes. Pulls a strand of hair from her face. Wraps it behind her ear.

"Maybe having that little bit of insight, that possibility that there might be some merit to my theory, maybe that will help you to understand the victim a little more, be a little more compassionate, choose better words, whatever it is, to make that moment in their life a little less painful," Mary adds.

I take the last bite of my sandwich.

"You want another one, Jimmy?"

"Naw. I'm good."

Mary stands to gather the plates and as she walks over to the kitchen sink, she says, "Jimmy, I think if you work on becoming aware of your own emotional responses, work to remove them from a situation, heck, just decide to distance yourself and not participate in the problem, I can't help but think you will help people weather their storm more easily, and that you will become the example for others to follow."

"I hope you're right, Mary."

I rise from my chair. "You've really been very generous with your knowledge. I want you to know how much I appreciate it."

"It's my pleasure. Just remember, Jimmy, change doesn't happen overnight. Takes time. You gotta work at it."

"Yeah. That's the tough part," I glance at my watch. "Shit. It's almost eight thirty. I had no idea it was so late."

"No problem, Jimmy. We talked about my favorite subject. I had fun."

"I've got an early start tomorrow, and I know you've got things to do as well."

"Let me walk you to the door," Mary offers.

Mary gives me a quick hug. I hug her back, and, as we separate, I look deep into soft brown eyes. They draw me in and something inside of me begins to move. I break away. We say our goodbyes.

TEN

February 9, 1989 – 8:53 PM

It's happening again – that connection.

I walk from Mary's doorstep. Find my way to the truck.

I don't want to feel Mary's life experience. It's none of my business. I don't want to know.

I get into the car and place my hands on the steering wheel, gripping it.

I stare through the window. Images of Mary fill my core. The depth of her loneliness. Her hunger for intimacy. The memory taunts me.

I start the engine.

How long has it been? Five, six years by now since that happened?

I shift gears. Shake my head.

You have to be careful around her, Hayden.

You can't let your guard drop for even a moment.

Not focusing on the drive, my mind wanders back to the day my intuition took me down that weary road.

I was shaken. So was Trevor. The father let go of the kid's hand. A car was barreling down the busy street, doing about thirty, thirty-five miles per hour. Hit the kid head on. Kid bounced off the windshield and lay sprawled on the street. There was no time to stop. It happened so fast. There was a crowd when we arrived. I gazed at the child. Couldn't be more than four years old. His white Izod shirt was flecked with dark brown and black marks. His navy-blue shorts spattered with blood. The father was taking no responsibility in the matter. Never thinking it might be his fault.

Bastard.

Mary met us at the doors of the emergency room. Our expressions reflected in the countenance of her face. The kid was comatose. She moved him along for treatment. Trevor walked back to the ambulance. I hung around. Mary walked toward me. Mouthed the words, "I'm sorry." She took my hand, looked deep into my eyes. They radiated concern. Channeled compassion. Her peace penetrated me and I was calmed. Then, like a sudden immersion under water, her loneliness devoured me, her desire for intimacy blending with me. I lingered to experience the knowing of it. I wanted to understand, but her pain was too great. It merged with me. And I knew what her life was like – what her relationship with her husband was like. It was like a movie burning into my soul. Her loneliness swept through me. I wanted to comfort her. Protect her. Save her.

Something's wrong!

Fear.

Break eye contact now!

I panicked. Removed myself quickly. "I'll catch you later, Mary." Confusion replaced compassion. Terror replaced grief. It was a quick stride back to the ambulance.

"What happened to you?" Trevor asked.

"Nothin'."

I remember being paralyzed in my thoughts, floating with each step taken toward the ambulance. It was one thing to feel these things in patients who were dying. It was quite something different to feel it in someone you knew. Someone you worked with. Someone you cared about. It felt like an invasion of privacy.

The guilt.

H-O-N-N-N-N-K!

Startled by the intrusion that jolts me to the present moment, I glance into the rear-view mirror, "What!" I yell at the mirror inside the safety of my car. The guy in the blue Ford pick-up truck is laying on his horn.

I lift a look to the stop light.

Green light.

I press my foot on the accelerator and finish the trek home. It's just a block away by now – another minute or two.

I sigh relief as I pull into the driveway. Unwittingly, I reach for the non-existent microphone to advise our communications center that we were in quarters only to realize that I wasn't in the ambulance. I was in my own vehicle.

" *'Gads.'* "

My mind is jumbled right now. Thoughts of invading Mary's privacy spinning in my head.

You didn't invade it. She let you in.

Yeah. Well...

I get out of the car and walk to the door.

I wonder if she knows what I did.

I mull over the distant memory. Try to feel for the answer. One doesn't come.

I wouldn't like it if she did that to me.

You wouldn't let her.

I fumble for the key in the darkness, slot it into the lock, and turn the tumblers to the right. I push the door open and flip the switch to turn on the light. I slam the door behind me and head down the dark hallway and into the bedroom. I don't bother to turn on that light. I plop down on the bed and fall back. I push the boots off my feet and let them fall to the floor. *I wonder if she knows.* The curiosity continues to dog me.

I wanted so bad to talk to Mary. Ask her why she stayed with her husband when she was so unhappy. *Maybe she's not unhappy. Maybe she's just unfulfilled.* Same thing, isn't it? Just seems to me that spending any part of your life with that kind of loneliness is such a waste. Why would anyone do that? Does she have kids? Is that the reason? Still. Even if she does, is she going to teach her kids to do the same thing? Stay in an unfulfilling marriage? Suffer the rest of their lives? Maybe it was about something bigger. Like values. Like family. Mary says everybody suffers something. Maybe on some level, we get to choose.

Hell, it's too much to think about right now.

I plump my pillows. Rest my head comfortably. Relax my mind.

Oh, but on a whole different level, she felt so good.

I let my mind escape. I drift off to sleep.

ELEVEN

February 10, 1989 – 5: 30 AM

I arrive at the station a half hour early. There's a slight chill in the air. Several crew members are still sleeping. Others are actively preparing for their departure. We exchange our "hellos," "good mornings," and "see ya laters."

I walk into the utility room that houses the keys to the ambulances and scan the key rack for Ambulance Seventeen. I remove the keys. Head downstairs to the ambulance. Collect the check-off sheet along the way. Conversations with Mary run like a ticker tape through my mind.

I open the driver's side of the cab, throw the check-off sheet on the passenger's seat, and start the engine. I let it run to warm up a bit then pull the lever to open the hood. I walk to the front of the vehicle.

I think of past behaviors, the caustic remarks, and the generous use of profanity that's become an acceptable part of the job.

The way we treat people sometimes...

I locate the dipstick to the transmission. Pull it out of the pipe. Check the fluid.

I'm going to change that – the way we treat people. I jiggle the dipstick back into the pipe. *I'm going find a way to set the standard.*

The dipstick slides in.

I reflect on Mary's words: *"Try not to participate in the problem. Work to distance yourself from the drama."*

I check the remaining fluids.

I just need to be aware of how I respond. Watch my emotions. Work to choose a better outcome.

Fluids are good. I slam the hood of the ambulance down tight. I check the tires.

"Roll call!" sounds throughout the station.

I glance at my watch. It's six a.m. I take the keys out of the ignition, collect the check-off sheet and run up the stairs to the main entry of the station house. I join Trevor at the table. "Hey, Trevor."

"Hey." Trevor takes a sip of coffee. "Did you finish the check-off sheet?"

"Yup."

Shuffling feet and the din of conversation serve as background noise to an otherwise quiet morning.

"Good morning, crew," the tinny female voice greets us over the radio.

"Good morning." The overlapping responses are anything but robust revealing a slow start to another day.

"Ambulance Forty-five. Schrant and Moss. Shop One-Fifty-One. Mile seven, one, eight, three, six, good morning," the dispatcher announces.

"Good morning."

"Good morning."

"Ambulance Seventeen. Hayden and Smith. Shop One-Twenty-Six. Mile seven, one, six, four, two, good morning."

"Good morning." The replies are simultaneous.

The dispatcher finishes with roll call. Someone turns on an episode of *Emergency!* I start to pour myself a cup of coffee when Bill shouts, "Breakfast anyone?"

TWELVE

February 10, 1989 – 7:40 AM

"Good breakfast, huh?" Al says as we enter the station.

"Yeah, time for a nap," I say.

"Get out," Bill says. "You just woke up."

"That was hours ago," I reply.

I plop my rear into the brown loveseat that faces the television set, close my eyes, and lean back in hopes of easing the discomfort in my belly. "I ate too much."

"Jimmy got a tummy ache," Al says with a sing-song tone.

I ignore him and turn on the television.

Whoooorrt! Whoooorrt!

"Christ."

"Channel Two. EMS. Stomach pain. Eight-

Twenty-One East Spence. Engine Twelve."

The phone rings. Al answers, "Station Eleven."

"Figures we'd get a call," I huff a snort. "I'll probably get this one too. My stomach hurts."

"Seventeen. Code three!" Al yells in my direction. "Somebody else got a tummy ache, Jimmy," he says, chuckling at the irony.

"Ah, hell." I thrust myself from the brown loveseat I had settled into so comfortably.

Trevor leads the way to the ambulance. He enters the cab and starts the engine before I reach the passenger side of the vehicle. "C'mon, Jimmy. Get in," he says.

"I'm comin'," My voice takes on a hard edge. I open the passenger door and pull myself in.

"Man. I hope this food settles soon." I rub my belly.

Trevor guides the ambulance onto Bethany Home Road. Takes a left at Twelfth Street.

Eighteen minutes later, we pull into a parking lot off Glendale Avenue.

"Oh, God. Another freakin' nursing home," Trevor says.

"I hate these calls." I scan our surroundings. "Park over there."

We park under a shade tree and exit the cab.

With gear in tow we approach the large glass doors of the entryway. Trevor pulls the bulky brass door handle and both doors swing open wide. We enter the lobby. The structure is huge – a good two-thousand-square-feet of uncompartmentalized space. Large round columns resembling Roman architecture are strategically placed to hold the vaulted ceiling. Old people hunched over walkers shuffle to and fro. Some sit on benches that are scattered throughout while staring aimlessly into open space – faces drooping, mouths open wide, the light in their eyes – gone. Chinks of sunlight cast a dull yellow hue over the room adding to the age and decrepitude of what the building personifies. We veer to the right and approach the concierge.

"Welcome." A cheerful voice from behind a dark brown desk greet us. "How can we help you, today?"

"We got a call for stomach pain," Trevor says.

"Oh, yes," she replies. "Room two-sixteen. Take the elevator up to the second floor and two doors down on your right." She indicates the elevator.

"Thanks," Trevor says.

We haul our equipment across the veined porcelain tile floor through the aged population. I push the elevator button. Doors open. We step inside and ride up to the second floor. A wisp of stale hot air hits us like a slap to the face.

We arrive at room two sixteen. Trevor knocks on the door. I detect a slight odor, like rotting beef.

The door opens. A putrid stench escapes. Trevor and I grimace as we step back.

"Yes?" Her voice quivers. She's short. Chunky.

Wiry salt and pepper hair piled on her head in a bun. Her pasty white skin has far outstretched her body.

"Someone here suffering from stomach pain?" Trevor asks.

"Yes. Please come in." Her voice is weak as though life has beaten her into submission.

We follow her through the small apartment.

"He's back here," she says.

She opens the door to the bedroom. I retch. Trevor gags. The pall of stench is unbearable, like maggot-ridden flesh that has been rotting for weeks.

A frail old man lies in a pool of vomit that resembles tossed coffee grounds.

"It's a G.I. bleed," I say.

Trevor ignores me. I glimpse the anger in his expression. The old lady retreats.

The threat of ejection resurfaces, and I can taste the remnants of digested breakfast in the back of my throat. I try to hold my breath. It's useless.

The old man moans. Face knots. I can see he's in agony. I don't care. I just want to dump him on the gurney and haul him off to the nearest hospital. They won't do anything for him anyway. I've seen it so many times with these old folks.

"Not doing so well, eh?" I huff an air of false concern.

"No." His voice is weak and shaky.

With hate-filled eyes, Trevor casts a glaring look

at the old man.

"GOD!" Trevor yells. His eyes water.

"Let's get him outta here," I say.

Trevor's expression supports that notion.

Trevor throws the air bag to the floor and removes the equipment needed to take the patient's vitals. I clean the old man up with a quickness of speed that mirrors the anger of inconvenience that I am currently housing.

The patient's breathing is shallow. Sketchy.

"Gimme the nasal prongs, Trevor."

Trevor pulls the nasal cannula and the oxygen tank from the airbag, passing them to me. I take the equipment and proceed in a manner which fully supports my intention of getting him off my agenda as quickly as possible.

I straighten the tubing of the nasal cannula. Holding the two nasal prongs with my thumb and forefinger, I insert each prong into its own nostril then wrap the tube that flails to the right around his right ear. I do the same for the left, then bring the tubes together down the front of his chest and hook the tubing to the oxygen tank. I catch a glimpse of emptiness in his fading blue eyes. It resonates a pain much greater than his physical discomfort.

A realization unfolds in my mind.

I'm being the problem I'm wanting to correct.

I draw back. Descend into shame.

"What's up, Jimmy?" Trevor's tone hints that he has sensed a change.

"Nothin'."

"Well, let's get moving," Trevor says.

"Yeah."

I peer into the eyes of the patient. I soften, and my muscles relax as I reconsider my approach.

"What's your name?" I ask while preparing the IV.

"Jones. Frederick Jones." He speaks with stuttered breath.

I insert the IV needle into his arm and tape it into place.

"Tell me what's going on, Mr. Jones." I place my hand on the side of his face. *He's cold.*

"My stomach hurts."

He winces.

"B.P. is ninety over fifty," Trevor says.

"Let's get him into a blanket and get his feet elevated."

Trevor throws a puzzled glance my way.

"What?" I say.

"Nothin'."

"Hand me the blanket."

I take the blue blanket and place it over the gurney in a fashion that will allow me to swaddle the patient.

"This oughta keep him warm," I say.

Trevor starts to slide the patient to the edge of the bed when I stop him. "Let's sheet lift him."

He glares at me. It's clear Trevor's pissed.

"Let's do it, Trevor. It will be less painful for

him. You take the two top corners, and I'll take the bottom two."

Trevor yanks at the corners of the sheet.

"Gently," I add.

His face twists with displeasure.

He takes the top two corners while I handle the bottom. We lift the patient from the bed and place him on the gurney. I wrap the sheet and blanket around the patient to swaddle him. Trevor gathers our gear.

We lead the gurney to the ambulance and lift it into the back of the vehicle.

"I'm gonna ride in back with him."

"Why?"

"To comfort him."

"What's gotten into you, Jimmy?"

"Nothing. Just drive, will ya? We gotta get him to the hospital."

I climb into the back of the ambulance. Trevor lumbers to the front. He guides the ambulance to the hospital. I check the patient's vitals while we exchange small talk. I hold his hand to comfort him.

Ten minutes later we arrive at the hospital. Trevor opens the doors to the patient's cabin. I release the gurney antlers. Roll the stretcher.

"I can't believe you secured the gurney," Trevor says as he rolls his eyes.

I don't bother to respond.

We remove the old man from the patient's

cabin. The mechanical folding legs expand. My hands jolt from an unnatural movement. I lift a look to Trevor. He's glaring at me, a sardonic grin stretches across his face. He let the gurney drop – just enough to rattle the patient.

I throw a look of "idiot" at him. He's irritated with me. I know it. I don't give a damn.

We roll the patient into the hospital.

"Whadda we got here?" a nurse approaches.

"G.I. bleed," I say.

" 'Kay. We'll take it from here," she says. She rolls him down the hallway.

Trevor and I start back to the ambulance when Trevor yells, "What the hell was that all about?"

"What was what all about?" I feign ignorance.

Trevor opens the doors to the back of the ambulance and we climb in. I pull a drawer, hand Trevor a towel. I collect the sheets.

"Don't give me that, Jimmy. You know exactly what I'm talking about. This business with sheet lifting the old dude and making sure the gurney is secured with the gurney antlers? Really? What the fuck is that all about?" Trevor stands. Arms crossed. Towel in one hand. I'm changing the sheets.

"Nothing," I say with a clipped tone.

"Don't give me that," Trevor repeats. "What gives?"

I ignore him.

"What gives, Jimmy?" Trevor yells.

I remain silent, wondering how the hell I'm

going to get him off my back.

"Jimmy." Trevor's tone is short and curt.

"I've just been having some trouble dealing with the agonies of life, lately. That's all. And I just think it's time we start being nicer to people."

"Whaaaat?" Trevor bursts into laughter. "You're kidding, right?"

"No. I'm not kidding."

I feel myself take on a look of "dead straight serious."

"Don't you ever think of the suffering, the tragedies we're engaged in nearly every day? And how these people deal? Or don't deal with it? Doesn't it faze you at all?"

"No, you pussy."

I catch a glimpse of his hurt.

He lowers his head, a resignation in his tone. "I can't, Jimmy. You know none of us can. It would send us to the mental institution and you know it."

"I know the suffering gets to you, Trevor. I see it in your face more often than you think. And lately it's been bothering me a little more, and I just think something should be done about it."

"About what?"

"The suffering, Trevor. The suffering. And the way we treat each other."

"And what do you think you are going to do about all the suffering, Jimmy? What do you think you are going to do about it? What? Are you out to save the world now? Do you really think sheet lifting an old man who is about ready to die is going to change the world? Do you really think that, Jimmy?"

"Well, sheet lifting the old man might not change the world today, but it could be the place to start and one thing is for sure..."

"What's that?"

"It changed the old man's world. It changed the level of suffering he had to go through, and it changed his world if but for only a moment. And maybe that's all that has to happen to start the process of change."

"Ah c'mon, Jimmy. Where are you going with this?"

"I don't want people to suffer any more. I don't want to add to their suffering. I want to make a positive difference in the lives of people I touch whether it's in the ambulance or elsewhere."

"Really?"

"Really."

The situation seems to require a moment of silence.

"Look. You don't have to participate if you don't want to, but I'm going to start treating people better, or at least I'm going to make the effort. If that means sheet lifting an old man that nobody cares about to make his life experience a little less painful, then I'm going to sheet lift the dude. We are all human, and we all suffer, and it's absolutely insane how we can be so cruel to each other and how cruel life can be to us, when it doesn't have to be that way. So I'm going to make a difference. I want to make a difference, okay?"

Trevor uncrosses his arms. Throws his towel to the floor. Crosses his arms again and leans against the door of the ambulance. I can feel his glare as I work. I ignore him, standing firm and holding my ground.

"You're a nut, Jimmy." Trevor chuckles, and he relaxes his posture.

I stutter a laugh.

"Why?"

"You think you're going to change the world."

I shake my head, lowering it. There is a tenderness in his jibing, and I know we're good. I love Trevor. He can be a little crass at times, but he's a good man.

"Let's head back to the station," Trevor says. There's resolve in the timbre of his statement. I warm to it.

We enter the cab, start the engine and alert the communication center that we're available. Trevor drives the ambulance toward the station. On the way, the radio sounds, "Ambulance Seventeen. Unconscious child. Four Twenty Nine South Oak. Easy Valley. Code three."

"Copy," Trevor answers. We turn our vehicle. Sirens blare. Lights flash. One more race against time.

THIRTEEN

February 10, 1989 – 8:55 AM

"Back here," the mother cries, tears welling in her blue eyes. She's short, thick around the middle, wearing pink capris and a black tee top. Her blonde hair hangs loose around the nape of her neck. We follow the young mother down the hallway where family pictures line the wall. She stops. Opens a door.

We enter the room decorated mostly in pink. A frilly white-laced runner spans the top of the dresser. Combs, hair brushes, a jewelry box, and miniature statuettes provide the landscape reflecting from the mirror. A rainfall of broken light casts its shadows through blinds that partially shade the room. The little girl lies on a bed decorated in pink and white. A collection of dolls and stuffed animals cluster at the foot of the bed.

Her body twitches, spasming uncontrollably.

"What happened?" I ask the mother while assessing the child's condition. She's frothing at the mouth, her eyes jerking wildly.

"I don't know," voice trembling, her face ashen. "She was outside playing with one of the neighbor kids when he ran into the house to get me. I went outside, and this is how I found my daughter. I brought her in here and called emergency."

"Looks like she's having some kind of seizure," I say to Trevor.

"Doesn't look like any kind of seizure I've ever seen," Trevor says.

I snap a pair of latex gloves into place. "Did we bring the suction cup?"

"I think so." Trevor rifles through the bag.

Using my fingers, I measure the distance between the corner of the mouth and the angle of her jaw. I reach into the airbag for an oral airway, select the appropriate size, then gently insert it in between her teeth to protect myself from injury.

Satisfied she is not gagging, I tilt the girl's head to the side. Her blonde hair shifts. I check the inside of her mouth for anything she might have vomited.

"Got it," Trevor says. He hands me what looks like a spray bottle. I insert the elongated tubing carefully into her mouth and squeeze the gun to extract the foam.

I eye the pretty pink dress that covers the length of her body.

I glance at the mother. "How old is your little girl?"

"She just turned four in November."

I turn to the patient.

"Look at how her eyes are jerking back and forth," I say to Trevor speaking in low tones. "What *is* this?"

"Man, I have no clue," says Trevor. "Looks like she's having a hard time breathing."

I remove the suction unit and the oral airway.

"Let's get a bag valve mask on her," I say.

Trevor hands me the oxygen tank.

"Is she going to be all right?" asks the frantic mother who is standing at the doorway.

"We're going to do everything we can, ma'am," I reply.

Trevor places the bag valve mask over the child's face. I hook up the oxygen tank.

"Hand me the stethoscope, will ya?" I say to Trevor.

I listen to her heart beat then take her pulse.

"Heart beat's irregular."

"I'll get the IV started," Trevor says.

"Looks like her tongue is swollen. Did she put anything into her mouth that she could have had an allergic reaction to?" I ask the mom.

"Not that I know of," she says.

"You wanna prep the arm?" Trevor asks.

"Sure. Hand me the tourniquet."

I tie a large plastic band just above the cephalic vein then turn to the air bag to pull the appropriate size needle and an alcohol swab. I tap the area just below the bend in her arm and swipe it with the alcohol.

Trevor steadies the arm while I gently insert the needle, securing it with medical tape.

"Hand me the arm board," I say.

I place the child's arm on the padded board to ensure the IV is secure. Trevor fixes the arm to the board with medical tape.

I place my hand on her forehead and with my index finger, peel the right eyelid, then the left. "Her eyes are still jerking." I pinch my lower lip. "Crazy."

"Let's get her on the gurney," Trevor says.

Mom steps aside while we run the gurney to the ambulance.

"I'll meet you at the hospital," she says.

Trevor opens the doors, and we lift the gurney into the back. I clamber up and slam the doors shut. Trevor guides the ambulance to the hospital.

I continue checking vitals.

"How long till we get to the hospital?" I ask.

"About five more minutes."

"Good. I wanna know what's wrong with her. I've never seen anything like this before."

We pull into the emergency entrance of the hospital where the medical team is waiting. We unload the gurney. Her body continues thrashing, mouth foaming, eyes jerking. Two nurse's aides run the gurney into the familiar sterile emergency room. Trevor walks to the nurses' station to give the report. I follow the patient.

I watch the medical team work. Nurse's aides transfer her to a hospital gurney. A nurse changes the IV bag. Another checks the kid's blood pressure. A respiratory therapist transfers the patient to hospital oxygen while the doctor assesses her condition. He places his hand on her forehead, lifts the little girl's eyelids, then takes the chest piece, and moves it around the patient. He listens. "Let's get her sixteen micrograms of IV Fentanyl and three vials of IV Anascorp stat."

Trevor joins me. "You ready?"

"Yeah. Let me ask the doc about her symptoms before we go."

I walk briskly to catch the doctor's attention. Trevor follows.

"Doctor Hochman," I say loud enough to catch his attention.

The stocky professional with a stolid expression spins around. He's middle aged and about my height of five foot eight. He wears a white medical jacket with a stethoscope draped around his neck. There's a slight bend to his posture.

"Hey, Jimmy. What can I do for you?"

"You know that little girl you just treated?"

"Yeah," the doctor replies.

"I was wondering what caused her symptoms."

"Scorpion sting."

"Scorpion sting?" I repeat to make sure I heard him correctly.

"Yup."

Trevor's gaze meets mine.

"No shit." I say.

"That's right, Jimmy. Those are the symptoms of a scorpion sting. I see it all the time. Muscles twitching. Shortness of breath. Swollen tongue. Roving eye movements. Most scorpion stings aren't serious, but they can be life-threatening for children of this age. Good thing you brought her in."

"I will say she had us stumped. We couldn't figure out what was wrong with her, could we, Trevor?"

"No. Jimmy thought she might have been having a seizure, but the way her eyes were jerking..."

"That's called nystagmus. It's where the eyes make repetitive, uncontrolled movements."

"Like that?" Trevor asks.

"Yes. They usually occur in a circular pattern, up and down or side to side, like you saw in the patient."

"Very interesting," I muse.

"Well, now you know," the doc says with a smile.

"Thanks, Doc."

"You bet." Doctor Hochman turns to walk to the charge station.

"Ready?" Trevor asks.

"Yeah. Let 'em know we're available."

We return to the ambulance. Trevor reaches for the mic.

"Ambulance Seventeen. Stabbing. Four Four Four One East Pueblo Avenue. East Valley. Code three."

"Copy." Trevor slots the mic in its pocket. We turn the ambulance around.

FOURTEEN

February 10, 1989 – 3:47 PM

We're in the ambulance. Been driving all day. It's brutal. Call after call. There's no letting up. They just keep coming. Chest pain. Unconscious male. Labor pain. A hit and run. A sports injury. Someone even ran over a cat.

I'm practicing my new attitude, keeping Mary's words close to me. I notice the difference it's making. My work seems more meaningful, more fulfilling. But my resolve is being tested. No break. No food. Breakfast was hours ago. I'm hungry. Tired. My bones weary, aching for a much-needed rest. I glance at my watch. *Three fifty-eight.*

"Ambulance Seventeen. Unconscious child. Five Fifteen South Marina Drive. East Valley. Code three."

We arrive on scene twenty minutes later. We walk up to the door of the house which is painted sky blue. A woman of Hispanic origin greets us. "He's in here," she says while guiding us to the bedroom. The woman walks away. We enter the bedroom where the little boy lies. Firefighters are already working on him. "Do you know what this is?" The thick muscular man with a mustache directs the question to his partner. "No. Haven't seen anything like this before," says the tall one with boyish features.

"Conversation has a ring of *déjà vu* to it," I say to Trevor.

We approach the child. His body is twitching. He's frothing at the mouth. His eyes jerk wildly.

"He's been stung by a scorpion," I announce. "Let's get an IV started."

"We're on it," the fireman with the mustache replies with a demeaning tone. "Looks like he's having some kind of seizure," he directs the statement to his partner.

Trevor and I trade glances.

"I'm telling you. It's a scorpion sting," I repeat.

"No. Doesn't look like a seizure to me," says the tall one.

"What? We don't count? You don't think we know what we're talking about?" I say.

The muscular man waves a hand of dismissal. The air of arrogance hits me like a slap to the face.

My eyes flick. I huff a snort of disdain.

"Then what could it be?" says the mustached fireman. His brow furrows.

"This one's got me," says the tall one – his face a question.

"It's a fucking scorpion sting," I repeat.

"Maybe he's having an allergic reaction to something," says the partner.

Like the movement of a shadow, anger forms, crossing my face, settling in.

"Fuck it, Jimmy. They don't give us any respect. Let's get outta here."

"Yeah. What do you say to a bunch of assholes who think they're better than us," I announce to Trevor.

Trevor takes my arm. "Let 'em handle this."

He guides me away.

"Those fucking assholes have no business treating us this way."

"They're assholes, Jimmy. What do you expect?"

"A little respect."

"Yeah. Well, don't hold your breath," Trevor says.

*****

February 10, 1989 – 4:39 PM
"Whaddya say we take a break?" Trevor says as we drive away from the scene.

"Sounds good to me. I could use the rest."

"Where to?"

My stomach is rumbling. I need something substantial.

"Let's go for some spaghetti."

Trevor rounds the corner. I relax into the seat of the cab. The sound of sirens deeply embedded in my psyche and the traumas of the day lodged in my bones. My stomach taunts me with hunger. I fold into the image of an indispensable, highly anticipated, break.

"Ambulance Seventeen. Difficulty breathing. East Valley. Apache. Code three."

"Fuck!" That was me.

Trevor reaches for the microphone. "Copy that." He slams the microphone back into its carrier.

Trevor turns the ambulance around. Screeching tires reflect the anger.

He floors the gas pedal, his expression stiff with tension.

"Trevor. It's probably just somebody with asthma needing a ride to the hospital."

It takes a minute to sink in.

His face relaxes "You're probably right. Don't know what I was thinking." He eases the gas pedal.

"Hospital's not that far. Shouldn't take long," I say.

"You're right, Jimmy."

My stomach grumbles. I ignore its request.

*****

February 10, 1989 – 5:07 PM

Tires crunch against the detritus of a pebbled dirt road as we guide the ambulance into the trailer park. Plumes of dust billow as I witness the undertakings of the panorama of filth we've just encroached upon.

Run-down trailer homes, deteriorated to the point of being uninhabitable, line the perimeter of the park. Their rusted structures, badly in need of paint and repair, are veiled in dust so thick it's clear no pride exists among these inhabitants. Doors are broken, windows boarded up, gaping holes in the structures. I wonder how in the world anyone could live like this.

The ambulance crawls forward.

A stray dog darts across our path. Trevor slams on the brakes. The dog's ribs protrude from under loose skin. It runs into a sea of abandoned vehicles – carcasses of rust strewn among overgrown grass that's dead and littered with garbage.

A child is crying.

I turn toward the sound. Dressed in a filthy tee-shirt and diaper, the child sits in a patch of dirt off the main path just outside one of the battered trailers. The kid can't be more than two years old. Flies buzz around matted black hair while snot streaks down the dirt-covered face. The scene reeks the epitome of filth.

Inching forward, Trevor guides the ambulance

down the dirt road.

The child cries louder and I wonder where the hell the parents are.

A niggling feeling sends a shiver up my spine.

I dart a glance to the right. Heavy-set men with loose fitting jeans and tatty tee shirts congregate around jacked-up vehicles. Long pony tails trail down the backs of men crusty with dirt – beers in one hand, cigarettes in the other. Their piercing eyes glare at us as the ambulance creeps down the road. Turning away, I peer at the spectacle of old cars and beat-up pickup trucks with faded paint and rusted body parts that are hugging their dilapidated structures.

The child is screaming.

A pack of dogs charge the ambulance.

Doors open. Bare-chested men with bellies hanging over belt buckles step out to see what is causing the commotion. Women dressed in loose-fitting clothes follow curious children. Their cold, calculating eyes bore into us.

And nobody gives a damn about the child.

"I don't like this place," I say. "Let's hurry and get the fuck outta here."

Trevor surveys our surroundings.

"I'm with you, dude."

We reach our destination.

We get out of the cab, gather our gear, and approach the deteriorated screen door that's partially open.

I note with disgust the filth that I'm surrounded in. The atmosphere of poverty is at a level I had never seen before.

Trevor knocks on the wall of the trailer.

A female approaches from within. She pushes the screen door. It creaks.

I stare dumbstruck at the woman who appears to be somewhere in her thirties. She could have been pretty. Her sandy blonde hair is long and looks like it hadn't been washed in weeks. The greasy strands cling to her forehead as if petroleum jelly were used to keep them in place. She's slender. Her braless tank top shows her every curve, an attractive body covered in filth. She stinks. And the cigarette that dangles from her mouth adds to the unpleasant odor and her shabby appearance.

"You here for my mom?" Her dialect is thick – ghetto.

"Is she having trouble breathing?" Trevor asks.

"Yeah."

"Then we're here for your mom."

"Follow me," she says. "She's in the back bedroom." Her manner of speech irks me. I'm becoming more irritable, more anxious the longer we are here.

We climb the rickety stair steps and follow the girl whose cut-off shorts reveal the rounded mound of fatty tissue on her derriere. The exposure implies an invitation for a potentially pleasing experience. Under normal circumstances, I might have been moved.

She stops at the entry of the hallway, points her arm to the closed door at the end. "She's down there in the bedroom at the end of the hall."

On our own, we walk down the short and narrow hallway. Clothing and general clutter line the walls, making it difficult for us to bring our equipment through. We pass by the kitchen. Dirty dishes pile high in the sink. Garbage and empty food boxes clutter countertops while flies feed off left-over food. An episode of *The Jerry Springer Show* blasts from somewhere in the trailer.

I shudder in disgust, anxious to get the job done and get the hell out of there.

I open the door to the bedroom.

The stench of human effluent slams me like a violent attack.

I gag, stumble back a few steps, catch myself, then pause to gather my senses.

Trevor cups his nose, retreats down the hall with a hushed cry of, *"GOD!"*

I approach the door again. Trevor's right behind me. I force myself to enter the room. My stomach plummets into an unrelenting darkness. I stare in horror at the vision burning into my retinas. My inner world shatters like shards of glass falling to the floor.

A muted cry of defeat ratchets up like a violent animal. I hold back the surging of tears.

Mouth agape, stupefied into silence, I struggle

to regain my composure, my brain working desperately to marry my expectation with the reality that is on display.

I inch toward the subject who has blinded me with despair. Trevor follows.

I stare at the unconscious woman, her eyes closed into tiny slits, a round bulbous nose planted deep within pudgy cheeks, her thin lips pressed into a straight line.

Anger burns from deep within as I recognize the futility of the work that lay ahead.

I toss a glance to Trevor. His gaze meets mine. He exhales a "Jimmy."

A seething fury sweeps over me as the reality that we may never get out of here crashes my mind.

I circle the patient. The walls of the bedroom close in as I gape at the monstrosity lying on the bed. The trauma of the moment screams hopelessness, and the energy of that word sucks the life out of me.

"How the fuck are we going to get this fat ass outta here?" Tears of anger fight to erupt. I struggle to hold them back. My voice trembles.

"Fuck. I don't know, Jimmy. But we gotta do something. She's about to go into cardiac arrest." Trevor gags. "God. No wonder she's having difficulty breathing."

She's huge. Her melon-sized head fuses with her shoulders. Images of pumpkins we carve at Halloween flash through my mind.

Her mid-section has to be a good five feet round and her elephant-sized legs stretch down to tiny fat feet reminiscent of the balloons with appendages that we used to blow up when we were kids.

"Call for backup, Trevor. There's no way we're going to be able to move her by ourselves."

Outrage spinning through me like a tornado.

She isn't just a mere inconvenience. She has shattered my plans, destroyed my night, put a horrible end to a long and gruesome day.

I move to the head of the bed to assess the situation. Her breathing is erratic, and the size of her body limits our ability to function.

I check for a pulse. It's futile. There's way too much fat everywhere.

"How the fuck am I going to intubate this tub o'shit?"

My outrage is met with silence.

Trevor begins chest compressions. It's clear we aren't getting a blood pressure cuff around those humongous arms, and the thought of starting an IV is a joke.

I watch Trevor as I work to solve the problem of intubating her. His hands sink deep into a sea of fat and I wonder if he's having any impact at all on the heart that's somewhere down there.

"How do you figure she got into this room?" Trevor says.

"Fuck if I know. There's no way she could have walked down that hallway or fit through that door, and I don't know how in the fuck we are we going to get her fat ass out of this trailer today."

"God. This place stinks!" I scream.

Trevor and I survey the room. Nothing's changed. There's no way to get her out.

"We're going to have to move her body to intubate her," I say. "That's the only way we're going to get medication to her since she's too fat to get an IV started."

"Good point," says Trevor.

Trevor and I strain to move her body, pushing, pulling, panting, and working chest compressions in between. Human excrement escapes from folds of puffy skin. The stench intensifies. I can't breathe. The horrific odor challenges my efforts to save her life as we work to straighten six-hundred pounds of morbid fat so we can get that tube down her throat.

"Holy fuck!" Bill cries as he and Dennis enter the room. The foul odor causes Bill's eyes to water. He swipes away the tears. "God. It's bad in here," he says with a tone of complete shock. I watch him retch. Dennis runs out of the room. Bill approaches Trevor to take over chest compressions. Trevor and I focus on straightening her body.

"Sorry, guys," Dennis returns wiping his mouth. "That shit caught me way off guard."

We all chuckle at his weakness even though there's nothing funny about the situation.

"How long do you figure she's been holed up in here?" Dennis asks as he tugs at the bottom of her legs pulling while Trevor and I push from the top.

"I don't know," I say as I struggle to shift her weight. "How long does it take to gain six-hundred pounds of ugly fat? A year or two?"

"Can you imagine living your life in a tiny room like this doing nothing but eating, sleeping, pissing, and shitting? And she was doing it all in this bed." Dennis gags.

Thank God I had no dinner. It would have melded nicely with the pungent odor that permeates the room now.

"Let's just figure out how to get this tub o' guts out of here." I'm unintentionally short.

Dennis takes over chest compressions giving Bill a break.

We finally get her body straightened out enough to get the bag valve mask over her head, a tube down her throat, and oxygen flowing to her lungs. I administer medication.

"Okay. Now how do we get this fat ass out of here?" I'm not holding back my anger. It's on full display. I don't care about anything other than getting her off my agenda. I want that done now.

We survey the room. It's barren. Just her, the bed, and a small brown dresser. And just enough room for a couple of EMTs.

"Through the window," Trevor says.

I evaluate the size of the window and guestimate it to be maybe a foot and a half square.

"You're kidding, right? You think a six-hundred-pound woman is going to go through that?"

"If we make it bigger she will," Trevor says.

The situation commands a moment of silence.

"We'd have to tear down the wall," says Bill.

Plucking my lip, I survey the room. Evaluate the alternatives.

"Let's do it," I say. "Let the daughter know."

Trevor and Dennis leave to collect the equipment needed for the teardown.

Bill continues with chest compressions while I call for additional backup.

"We still have to find a way to transport her to the ambulance," says Bill through short rapid breaths. "There's no way she's going to fit on the gurney."

"Yeah, I know," I reply. "I'm thinking we tie two backboards together and carry her on that."

The sound of shattering glass cuts the air as Dennis and Trevor start the teardown. The wall is easily torn from the deteriorated structure.

Curious minds gather outside, people inching closer as the wall comes down.

"Great. Just what we need," I say with a grating tone.

"Put out those cigarettes or you'll blow the place up!" I shout.

"Freakin' idiots," I say to Bill.

"Hey, Jim... Bill. What's going on?" Al asks as he and Steve enter the room. "God. Stinks in here."

Steve gags. Al covers his nose. I watch as they grapple with the pungent odor that swallows them.

"We've got six hundred pounds of fat here who's having difficulty breathing and we need you to help us get her to the hospital. Clearly, she's too big for the gurney, so we figure we put two backboards together and carry her through that doorway." I point over to Trevor and Dennis who are finishing up the opening. "And then we need the manpower to carry her."

"Gotcha," replies Al. "You want us to get the backboards set up?"

"Yeah."

"We're on it."

"I'm not looking forward to this," I say to Bill. "It's going to take an act of God to get her out of here, and I don't think she's going to make it."

"I agree. But with the six of us, we should be able to hoist her, don't you think?"

"Hell. I don't know. Just because you were a world heavy weight champion in wrestling…"

"We got the backboards," Al interrupts as he and Steve bring the large yellow boards through the new entryway.

"Let's get them ready to go!" I call out.

We tie the two boards together with the spider strap to create an area large enough to place her. Steve positions the backboards near the bed.

"We're going to need to roll her enough to get the backboards under her," I say. Bill joins me to cover the mid upper section of her body.

"Trevor. You wanna take the lower mid-section? Dennis can take the hips."

"Sure."

"Okay. Ready?"

"Yup," says Dennis.

"On the count of three. One. Two. Three. Pull."

We pull. Pull on her limbs. Pull at her sides. Pull on her clothing. The strain is unbearable. We pant like spent horses.

"It's not working, Jimmy!" Bill yells and releases his hold. We let her drop.

I pinch my chin as I think a moment.

"Okay. Al, why don't you pull with Dennis and Trevor. Bill, you and I can push her from her backside. We just need to make sure there's enough room for Steve to get the backboards under her. Steve. Do you think you can handle the backboards by yourself?"

"I don't know." Steve eyes the six-foot-long boards that are about a foot and a half wide each. "I'll give it a shot."

He drags the backboards over to the side of the bed.

Trevor takes hold of her upper arm. Dennis positions his hands on her waist. Al latches onto the thighs.

Bill and I stand ready to push from her backside.

"You guys ready?" I ask.

"Yeah," they reply.

"Okay. On the count of three. One. Two. Three. Lift."

They pull.

We grind our weight into the push, exhaling heavy breaths, rivulets of sweat rolling into our eyes. I swear it'd be easier to lift a two-ton truck.

"Hurry, Steve. Get the backboard under her!" I yell with a groan.

Steve lifts the backboards and places them on the bed, shoving them under the body. He scrambles to position them so that she is somewhat centered.

"Hurry, Steve," Bill grunts.

Steve pushes harder until he can't push any more.

"Okay. Drop her," Steve hollers.

We let the body fall. I dab my eyes with the corner of my shirt.

"Let's get her secured."

The six of us work to center her body.

"Tape her head, Bill. I'll tie her hands."

Trevor positions her legs.

"She's ready to go," says Bill.

"Trevor, Dennis, and Al, you take her right side. Bill, Steve, and I will take her left."

After a beat, "You ready?" I ask.

"We're ready," says Trevor.

"On the count of three," I say.

"One, two, three." We lift. Arms quiver. Grunts

escape. Like Arnold Schwartzenegger lifting weights, but without the training. Our arms shake as we hoist her into the air. We leverage our shoulders for balance.

"Shit. Her fat is hanging over. I'm about to lose her!" I yell with labored breath. I struggle to keep her suspended.

My hold wobbles. My legs ache. The weight is unbearable. We stumble to the ambulance.

Damned William Toms. White trash too stupid to move. I struggle with the cargo. "MOVE!" I yell. They trail us like a pack of dogs looking for food.

We arrive at the ambulance. Trevor balances his end of the backboard on his right shoulder to open the door to the passenger's cabin.

We maneuver the backboards into the patient's cabin. Huffing, we all push with every ounce of muscle we have until we hear a thump that tells us she's as far back as she can go. Panting heavily, we relax.

The foot of the backboards jut out just enough to keep the doors from closing.

Hands on hips, I turn a half circle. "Fuck! Fuck! Fuck! Fuck! Fuck!" I turn again to face the problem. We're all staring, trying to figure out a solution.

"GET BACK!" I scream at the crowd that has increased in size.

Surprised by the outburst, they jump back.

"Let's get her off the backboards," I say.

"How you goin' to do that?" Al asks.

"Hell, I don't know," I shoot back. "Should be easy enough just to roll her off."

"She's taking up the whole back of the patient's cabin now. How we gonna get someone in there to unsecure her?" Bill asks.

"What's our other option?" I say. "Unload the whole kit and caboodle and unsecure her on the ground?"

"Then we'd have to get her back up into the cabin," says Al. "Better to roll her off while she's in there."

"Let's push her as close to the side of the cabin as possible. Might give us a little more room to work with," I say.

We push. She inches closer to the side. We grunt, then pant.

"Who wants to be the one to unsecure her?" I ask.

No one answers. They stand around like useless parts.

"Fine. I'll do it."

I climb into the patient's cabin, edging my way around her body.

I remove the tape and gauze. Her arms fall to her sides.

"I'm going to need help rolling her," I say.

"I'll help." Bill climbs into the cabin. It's a tight fit.

Bill and I roll her to her side while Trevor, Al, and Dennis push on her from outside of the cabin.

Steve yanks at the backboards, jerking and wiggling until they break free. Steve stumbles back. Her legs flop over the threshold. Bill and I release our hold. She rolls to the floor.

"Jesus, she's heavy," Bill comments with a heavy breath.

"Now we gotta get the rest of her inside," I say. I glance around the cabin. "I don't think it's big enough."

"We already know that," says Bill.

"You guys wanna figure out how to get her humungous ass and legs in here? Bill and I will pull."

Without responding, Dennis and Steve lift her legs so that Trevor and Al can push on her hips. Bill and I pull on the upper portion of the body, angling her so as to make the best use of available space in the patient compartment. We inch her in. Al and Trevor angles her hips so that Dennis and Steve can position her legs and feet in any way that would allow them to shut the doors and move on.

She's packed in the patient's cabin filling up the entire back of the ambulance, like dirty laundry stuffed into a duffel bag only smelling like a sewage plant.

There's very little room for Bill and me to operate. Bill lies on top of her to continue with chest compressions. My knees are shoved up to my chin making it difficult to administer medication.

Trevor enters the driver's side of the cab while

Dennis enters from the passenger side. Steve and Al head back to the station. Trevor starts the engine, slams the gear shift into drive and turns the ambulance around. Driving to the hospital, he pulls the microphone out of the carrier and alerts them we are on our way.

"She is not going to make it," I say to Bill.

"That's a foregone conclusion."

We continue resuscitation efforts.

"God, she stinks," I complain.

"Yeah. Stink doesn't even begin to describe it," Bill says. He gags.

"We're almost at the hospital," Bill says.

"Good. I can't wait to unload this tub of shit."

Bill pulls out the stethoscope – moves it around her chest.

"I got a heart rate."

"Shit. You're kidding."

"No, man. I got a heart rate."

"Well, I'll be damned. I guess the meds worked," I say.

We pull into the emergency entrance of the hospital to find doctors and nurses waiting. A swarm of aides rush to the ambulance to help unload the patient. They transfer her from the back of the ambulance onto their gurney like it's "business as usual." I'm amazed by how easily they handle her. The aides wheel her into the hospital, and doctors and nurses begin treatment.

Heart rate's a fluke. She ain't gonna make it. I

shrug indifference.

I walk to the nurses' charge station and give my report.

Trevor joins me. "You about done?"

"Yeah." I wrap up the report and we walk to the ambulance.

"I dread the thought of cleaning that cabin," I say with a little venom in my tone.

"Let's just get it done, Jimmy. The quicker we get that done, the sooner we can get outta here."

"I know."

"Hey, man, thanks for the help," I yell to Dennis and Bill as we pass them by.

"Yeah. The next time you get one like that, call someone with a tow truck," Bill says.

"Or a snow shovel," says Dennis.

"Yeah, yeah, yeah, like it snows in Phoenix," I say.

"At least you don't have to clean the ambulance," says Trevor.

"Thank God," says Bill. "I don't think I could handle another second breathing in that shit."

"Lucky us," Trevor says.

We arrive at the ambulance. I hesitate to open the doors.

"Catch you 'round," Trevor says to Bill and Dennis.

I open the doors. I gag at the odor that slaps me in the face again.

I peruse the back of the ambulance to see what

damage has been done.

Remnants of fecal matter and dried urine are scattered throughout. Blood, chunks of hair, torn flesh, and other unidentifiable substances.

I get a sinking feeling.

"Did we really treat her that bad?" I ask Trevor.

"She deserved it." His tone is clipped.

I stare at the damage. It's pretty bad.

"I think we were too rough on her," I say to Trevor.

"Forget about it, Jimmy. She's a big fat piece of shit, literally. All that work we did? What'd we put in? Four? Five hours of hard labor? And for nothing. You know she's just gonna die."

The memory of a promised dinner flashes through my mind. My stomach growls.

"All that work for nothin'," Trevor repeats.

He's got a point.

I stare at the excrement, breathing in the pungency. Anger and remorse pitted inside of me like two north poles.

I certainly didn't employ any of the principals I learned from Mary.

Another sinking feeling.

I peer into the back of the ambulance.

If I could just take a hose to it.

FIFTEEN

We slam the doors. Head toward the front of the ambulance as we get ready to leave the hospital. We climb in. Trevor starts the engine.

"Where to?" he asks.

I check my watch. It's ten after ten. I'm so tired. I can barely keep my eyes open. I lean my head against the headrest. Close my eyes. There's a hollowness in my stomach.

"I need to eat," Trevor says. "You hungry?"

"Naw. I can't eat just yet. I still have the taste of shit in my mouth."

He lets a minute pass. "Let's go check on the cat."

My voice is raspy with exhaustion. "You mean the one we tried to save earlier today?"

"Yeah."

"You hate cats, Trevor."

"I know. But I'm curious. I want to know if we saved it. It'll only take a minute."

My voice takes on a dream-like quality. "Fine. We can probably eat after that if you want."

Trevor takes a right at the light.

Visions of the black cat with white paws and a white streak running down its nose swim through my mind.

"That was some call." I exhale.

"What was some call?"

"The cat."

"That was no call," Trevor's speech is sluggish. "We stopped because we saw a bunch of people standing 'round what I thought was an injured party."

"It was an injured party," I say with a slight chuckle. "Just not the kind of party you were thinking it was."

I rub my eyes. "You should have seen the look on your face when you discovered it was a cat."

Trevor snorts.

"Yeah. Well. All those cars pulled off to the side with their emergency blinkers blinking, you woulda thought it was a person, not a freakin' cat," Trevor says.

"You turned the ambulance around so fast."

"And *you* wanted to ease the cat's suffering. That cat didn't have a chance in hell of making it. It was in such bad shape."

"I know."

Trevor breathes a heavy sigh. "Man, I'm tired."

"Yeah. Me too."

I rest for a beat.

"You know. I couldn't just leave the cat to die."

"You're such a wuss, Jimmy."

My stomach rumbles.

"The cat had a heart rate."

"The cat was pretty much dead," Trevor corrects. "You knew that by the way its chest was moving up and down, like it was breathing."

The unnatural movements flash in my mind. I knew the brain hadn't received the message yet. That's what gave me hope.

"To tell the truth, I was surprised that the cat made it to the hospital," I say.

"Yeah. I know. We treated it like our life depended on it. You got the pediatric equipment to intubate the cat and put that bag valve mask over its head. I c-spine immobilized the darn thing. I think we did a pretty good job."

"Maybe."

I pause for a moment.

"We sure did draw a crowd," I say.

"Yeah, that *was* some crowd," says Trevor. "I

don't think anybody expected us to work on the cat the way we did. I mean, we were really working to save its life."

"That's for sure. Vet was a miracle worker, too," I say.

"I guess we'll find out how much of a miracle worker she really was here in just a few minutes." Trevor says.

Whooort! Whooort! Channel Two. EMS assignment. Rollover. East Valley, Casa Grande. Code three."

"Ah, fuck." Trevor comments.

My stomach rumbles. Anger rises. I push it down.

*****

February 10, 1989 – 10:28 PM

The roar of the hurst tool dissecting metal cuts through the silence of the desert while flashing red lights mar the pristine beauty that can be seen under the bright white light towers.

We stop the ambulance, collect our gear, and run toward the eyesore that violates the peaceful landscape.

I inhale its beauty. Overgrown patches of yellow grass married with grayish stubs of shrubbery dot the sandy-colored earth. The Arizona foothills are non-existent against the blackness of the night. For one who's not accustomed to it, it can be an eerie feeling.

"What happened?" I ask a police officer who is monitoring the situation.

"Kids screwing around." He writes something on his notepad. "The driver lost control of the car."

I survey the wreckage.

The passenger side of the brown Mazda Roadster is badly crumpled and lodged into the interior of the car. Firefighters work the hurst tool to cut away the metal that holds the dead body.

Trevor and I run to the driver's side of the vehicle.

I pull on the handle. The door opens. He's a large man. Muscular. The bouncer type. I hook my arms under the armpits and work to pull him out of the car.

"Ow. Watch the arm," he orders.

I oughta drop you right now.

I'm tired. Not in the mood for this shit.

Trevor moves around to catch the lower portion of his body. We place him on the backboard.

"His arm is broken," says Trevor.

"Damn right," the patient barks.

My mind reels with his patronizing tone.

"And you'd better not hurt it," he adds.

Prick.

I tape his head.

"What are you doing?" The victim whines.

I give him a sharp look.

Trevor straps him to the board.

"Get me off this thing." The victim squirms.

My thoughts spin. Mary's words pop into my brain. *Don't become one with the problem.*

"Hold still," I say with a sharp tone.

He pauses.

Fucking selfish bastard.

I take his vitals. Trevor works to stabilize the broken arm.

"What are you doing?" the patient demands.

"We're trying not to break the other arm," Trevor shoots back.

"You're hurting me," he complains.

Trevor glares at him. "You have no idea what we could do if we really wanted to hurt you."

I bandage his cuts.

"Shit stings."

I'm not liking him anymore, but Mary's words haunt me. I'm resolved to keeping my care compassionate.

Trevor prepares the IV.

"What are you gonna do with that needle?" the patient calls out.

Trevor inserts the needle with a quick sharp thrust causing the patient to cry out. I catch a glimpse of Trevor's reaction. His stomach spasms with a suppressed chuckle.

I smile.

"You did that on purpose," the patient accuses. "I'm going to report you."

I roll my eyes.

Trevor secures the IV needle with medical tape.

We glimpse the police carrying the dead body away from the scene.

"Is that all you care about is yourself?" Trevor turns to the patient.

The patient's face twists with anger.

"You hurt me."

"I see," says Trevor. I can tell he really doesn't give a shit.

"You ready, Jimmy?"

"Yeah."

"Let's get him loaded into the ambulance."

We lift the backboard. Place it on the gurney.

"How's Julie?" the patient demands.

I look deep into his eyes.

"She's dead." I say with a level tone. "You killed her."

*****

February 11, 1989 – 1:08 AM

"Weren't we at this hospital just a couple of hours ago?" My voice strains.

"Yup." Trevor shuts the engine down.

"God. I must be tired."

"You should be." Trevor's voice is raspy. Weak. "We've been at this since about seven thirty this morning. What time is it now? One?"

I check my watch. "Yeah. It's quarter after."

My bones ache. My stomach – raw.

We deliver the patient to the medical team. They assist with transferring the patient to their equipment. He's quiet now. The news must have hit him pretty hard.

Trevor and I stroll to the nurses' station. There's minimal activity. It's the middle of the night.

"Weren't you here a little while ago?" a nurse asks.

"Yeah," I say.

"I'm gonna give the report, Jimmy."

Trevor lumbers away.

I turn to the nurse. "You know that patient we brought in earlier today? The one who had difficulty breathing?"

"Yeah."

"What happened to her?"

"Oh. She's recovering in ICU."

"What?" I snort a chuckle. "You're kidding."

"No, I'm not."

"I didn't think she'd make it."

The nurse smiles. "Well, she did. We're pretty good at what we do around here."

I feel my face crimson. "Oh. I didn't mean to imply..."

"I know you didn't," the nurse cuts in. "You want to see her?"

"Yeah. I'm just curious."

"She's down the hall to your right."

"Thanks."

I walk down the stark white hallway and step

into an equally stark white room where chunks of equipment made of stainless steel cut into the landscape. Lights are on and it's bright inside, like it's the middle of the day.

The massive woman is sitting upright in her bed. She's been extubated and is breathing on her own. I stare in wonderment. An episode of *The Jerry Springer Show* sounds from the television set that is anchored to the wall. She's hooked into an episode. The husband is having an affair with the wife's sister.

"How are you doing?" I ask loud enough to be heard over the sound.

She looks my way. Her face takes on a blank expression.

"My name is Jim. I brought you in earlier today, and I am in complete shock that you are sitting there looking at me. I really thought you were going to pass away."

She throws a puzzled look.

There's a drawl in her dialect. "I'm sorry, but I don't think I know you."

"I'm one of the EMTs that helped get you to the hospital in an attempt to save your life. Looks like we succeeded." I grin.

She stares at me. Her expression is a look of trying to put the pieces together.

She turns the sound of the television all the way down.

"Well, you really gave us a go," I continue. "I'm

glad to see you are doing okay."

"Yeah, I'm doing okay. Thank you for whatever you did. I'm so sorry I don't remember you."

"Oh. Not to worry," I say.

A beat.

"Do you remember anything?" I ask.

"No," she shakes her massive head. "Nothing."

Her mind is searching. Her eyes flick up.

"Wait. I do remember something."

I arch an eyebrow. "Good. What do you remember?"

"I remember somebody calling me a fat ass."

My stomach drops.

"He called me a fat ass a few times."

It drops again.

She fiddles with her fingernails. Tears well. She turns her head.

The exhaustion in my body takes a new place in my awareness.

I fill with remorse.

Her tears take their own form of vengeance.

She weeps.

"He's right, ya know."

Tension builds. The weight of her words hit me like a wrecking ball.

"And what my life has become." She sobs.

Rivulets of sweat form on my brow.

"How could I have let myself get like this?" she blubbers.

She swipes at tissues sitting on her tray.

Gravity is pulling at the weight of my body. My blood thrums through me like pops of fireworks bursting into the sky on Independence Day.

She plants her face square in the tissue and blows.

"I hate myself," she bellows. "I hate myself for letting me get this way."

"Now. You shouldn't talk like that," I say.

She swipes at more tissue. She sobs convulsive sobs. Her massive stomach bounces with each breath.

How could I have been so cruel?

"How could I have let myself get like this," she bawls.

God. I hate myself. How could I have been so stupid, so heartless?

"W-h-y-y-y-y?" she cries out.

The guilt. Like ants to candy.

I struggle.

She weeps.

The sobbing subsides. She sniffles.

"Yes. He called me a fat ass several times," she repeats.

I don't know what to do.

"I just hate myself," she says.

I can't take it anymore.

"Why did I let myself get this way?" she says.

"That was me."

She weeps a little more.

"I'm so sorry," I add.

She pulls a tissue. Wipes her eyes. Blows her nose.

"What was you?" she chokes back tears.

"That was me who called you a fat ass."

Her eyes are puffy. Her nose, red. Her expression, vacant. She doesn't comment.

To see how I hurt her buries me in shame.

"I will never be that insensitive again. I am so sorry," I repeat.

She sniffles, fiddles with tissue.

"I deserved it," she says with a tone of resignation.

"No you didn't. No one deserves to be spoken to that way. I was wrong."

She turns away.

"No. You're right. I am a fat ass."

"I might have chosen kinder words. I'm so sorry I didn't."

Sniffling, she peers at me.

"Thank you for what you did," she says. "You saved my life, and I thank you for that."

"You're welcome."

She turns her attention to the tissue.

"And it looks like you are going to be just fine," I say.

I can see her mind is occupied.

"Okay," I say. I pad to the doorway.

She raises her head. "Thank you for checking on me."

I stop and turn to face her.

"Thank you for caring," she adds.

She pats her eyes with tissue and attempts a smile.

I walk over to her. I lean in to give her a hug.

"Promise me we won't meet like this again."

She lifts a look.

"Promise me," I repeat.

"I promise."

SIXTEEN

February 11, 1989 – 2:20 AM

We arrive at the station. I check my watch. Twenty after two. It's the middle of the night.

I'm so tired – dog tired. I barely have the energy to walk. Same with Trevor. Both of us, quivering with exhaustion.

I shuffle my way to the bed.

Every muscle, every bone in my body aches with a demand for rest.

I collapse onto the bed. Ignore the cry for food. Dismiss the need to undress.

I fold into the peaceful, uninterrupted stillness of a full body sleep. Deep, restful, glorious, dead weight sleep.

"Ambulance Seventeen."

A slight stir. I barely cock an ear.

Silence.

I sink back into that deep quiet stillness.

"Ambulance Seventeen."

An atrocious assault.

"Ambulance Seventeen. We have a call for you."

I wake to a state of semi-consciousness. Glance at my watch. Two forty-three AM.

"What is it?" I slur.

"You need to take Mr. Jones back to the nursing home."

"F-U-U-U-U-U-U-U-C-K!" bounces off the walls.

Trevor.

"Ambulance Seventeen?"

"Yeah." My voice strains.

"You need to take Mr. Jones back to the nursing home."

" 'Kay." Every muscle, every nerve in my body quakes as though electrical shocks are detonating throughout my limbs.

"Ambulance Seventeen."

"I'm comin'!"

I force my body to move. The weight of the exhaustion fights mercilessly to keep me in bed.

I manage to push myself upright. I shake my head to gather my senses.

I'm numb. I flex my hands to get circulation moving.

"Ambulance Seventeen."

"I'm up."

I hope somebody stole the ambulance.

I push myself off the bed, work boots still on my feet.

I lumber through the great room, down the stairway. Trevor joins me. We're groggy, walking in our sleep. I don't want to go. Neither does Trevor. His expression screams it.

We get into the ambulance and drive. The vibration of trundling tires shimmies through my body like the drumming of a tuning fork.

We pull into the driveway of the emergency entrance. Park the ambulance. Trevor shuts the engine down. We gather our equipment and enter the hospital.

"We came to collect Mr. Jones," I say to the nurse seated at the charge station.

I glance at the clock on the wall. It reads five minutes after three.

"Oh yes," replies the heavy set, middle aged woman dressed in white. She lifts a hand and points. "He's just down the hallway."

Alert now, I eye the familiar blue blanket.

"Bastards," I say to Trevor. "They didn't even touch him."

"What'd you expect, Jimmy?"

"I was hoping this one would be different." Disappointment weighs on me. "I just thought, if they could see we invested in the old man..."

"You're a dreamer."

We approach the gurney.

"You ready to go home, Mr. Jones?" I ask.

He lifts a glance. Doesn't respond.

Trevor and I take hold of the sheet. We transfer him from the hospital gurney to ours and roll him to the nurses' station to discharge him. We don't bother giving a report.

"I'm going to ride in the back with him," I say to Trevor.

He rolls his eyes. We load the patient into the back of the ambulance. I climb inside.

I sit beside Mr. Jones and take his hand.

"How are you doing?"

"I'm okay," the barely audible reply is unsteady.

His face is drawn and heavily spotted. He's gaunt, pale, pasty white.

I place my palm on his forehead. He's still cold.

"They didn't do anything in the hospital," he says.

I peer into moist blue eyes. They're streaming with pain. His face stiffens.

"I'm sorry. I'm going to do everything I can to make you comfortable."

"I know they sent me home to die," he says with noted effort. "I'm a burden on society anymore, a useless old man that nobody wants."

What do I say to something like that?

"I wish I would just die," he says in between breaths. "Get it over with. If I wasn't such a coward, I'd do it myself."

"Hey, guy. Don't talk like that. It's not good for the soul," I say soothingly.

"I'm sorry," The old man's voice is hoarse, weepy. "I don't mean to unload on you. It's just been such a shitty life and now this."

He knots his face.

"There must have been something good in your life."

I read a silent question in his expression.

"Yes," he says – his voice weak. "I've done things in my life that I would have never dreamed possible."

"What kind of things?"

I check the fluids in his IV.

"Well," he says, breathing heavily. "I got my high school diploma, for one."

His brows pinch.

"I know no one would think that was a big deal."

A pause.

"But it was for me."

Fluids are low. I adjust them to required levels.

"Why was it such a big deal?"

His voice quivers. "Because no one in my family ever went past the tenth grade."

He takes a breath. "No one ever graduated from high school."

"Wow. I thought graduating from high school was something that's pretty much taken for granted."

"Maybe for most, but not for me."

I check to see that the IV needle is secure.

"I wanted a high school ring."

He takes a breath.

"To symbolize my accomplishment...

I worked a full-time job at nights."

"What kind of work did you do?" I ask.

"Worked in a factory, wrapping packages of paper, like the notepads people use for school and in the office."

"Yeah?"

"Piece work." His breathing – heavy and labored.

"Saved my money to buy that ring and finish high school."

I check his pulse.

"That ring meant so much to me. I wore it all of the time."

"I would imagine. Do you still have it?"

"Yes, but only by a miracle through God."

"Why? What happened?"

I pull out my stethoscope and place the metal chest piece on him.

"One day a bunch of us went swimming by the rocks in Lake Michigan, in Chicago, where I am from." He takes a minute to catch his breath. "I came up out of the water and the ring was gone. I was crushed. I had lost the ring." He let out an audible sigh. His voice wavers. "You ever been to Chicago?"

"No. Can't say that I have."

He winces.

"Then you can't appreciate, that considering

where I lost that ring, the probability of finding it was pretty much nonexistent."

"You're probably right." I smile.

I remove the stethoscope.

"I was so distraught."

He continues speaking, as though his brain is slowly calibrating every word. "One day I was riding on the city bus. An old school buddy happened to be on that same bus so I sat next to him. I told him my story of how I lost the ring. I was so upset. He tells me he's got a friend who found a high school ring in that same location. Says he'll ask him about it. Turned out to be my ring."

"You're kidding."

"No, I'm not." His voice is quavering.

"I'm the oldest of six kids."

"We all grew up in foster homes." His face flutters. "I'm the only one in my family who actually made it through high school." He says with shortened breath. "I earned a college degree and made something of myself in corporate America." He grasps his stomach, wincing. "That ring symbolized the first and most important accomplishment in my life."

"That's an amazing story."

I check his heart rate. It has increased.

"Yup. But it all went to hell in a hand basket when I decided to become an entrepreneur."

"How do you mean?"

"I got tired of being an employee."

He exhales a sigh.

"I was drawn to the promise of wealth that so many so-called experts preach about.

"I listened to those motivational speakers.

"Did what they told me to do...

Worked like a dog."

His eyes take on a vacant stare.

"Rather than create wealth and freedom, I created poverty and slavery."

I arch an eyebrow. "Slavery?"

"A slave to money." He takes a raspy breath. With a wobbly voice he continues, "Spent thirty years of my life trying to find the magic bullet that would get me what they said I could have, and all I ended up with is a broken down body that no one wants anything to do with, including myself."

He pauses to reflect.

"Yup, instead of achieving the American dream, I ended up in the American nightmare."

He catches his breath. "Son, don't listen to those people who say you can have everything you want. You can't."

"Why do you think you ended up in the American nightmare?"

"If I knew the answer to that question, I'm sure the ending of my life would be much different."

Continuing in his raspy, wheezy cadence, "The only thing I can trace it to are the choices I made." He winces again. "I got here because of the choices I made in life, and, apparently, every choice I made was a bad choice as it took me in the opposite direction of where I wanted to go. I could never figure out why."

I wonder if this has anything to do with that vibrational stuff Mary was talking about.

I add medication to the IV.

"And I did fall in love once," he says in a slower voice as he recollects his experience.

"Yeah? With the woman who answered the door back at the nursing home?"

"Oh no," he says. "That's my sister."

There's a moment of silence.

He smiles. "She'd have nothing to do with me."

He clears his throat.

"It was an experience I will never forget."

He continues, "Through her I got to discover what true, genuine love is, and for the first time, I fully understood the loneliness of man. I knew love and loneliness in a way I had never known before."

"Is that a good thing?" I ask.

"I'm not so sure. It would have been good if we could have come together. But she made a different choice."

"I see."

I'm curious as to why Mr. Jones is so willing to share his tattered memories with me. I guess I am a bit responsible considering my probing questions. And he has convinced himself he's going to die. He made that clear at the beginning. So, is this why he's sharing? Because he knows he's going to die? I hear people's lives flash before their eyes at the moment they're facing death. Maybe this is another version of the same thing.

"You seem like a nice young man. Would you like some advice?"

"Sure."

"Save your money."

A pause.

"Take a portion of it and put it in something that you will not touch under any circumstances until you're the age of fifty-five or older." Speaking in truncated sentences, he continues. "Life is cruel, and it doesn't get better as you age, especially if you're broke." He pauses to take a breath. "There's an old saying and it goes something like this: Love makes the world go round but it's money that pays for the trip."

"Oh, I like that saying. Where'd you get it from?"

"Don't remember, but it's one that was permanently seared into my mind. It's the phrase that kept me going." He smiles.

The old man shifts.

I check to secure his blanket.

"If you save your money and things go sour, you'll have something to fall back on."

"I do save my money, but I don't have a savings I will never touch. I'll have to look into that."

"Do. It's important."

He pauses.

"Make good choices in your life. Lead with your heart and evaluate with your brain. That's why you have one of each." He blinks.

"Don't listen to those people who say God wants you to be rich and He wants you to be happy." He clasps his stomach. Winces. "God doesn't care if you're rich or happy. If He did, everyone who wanted to be rich and happy, would be rich and happy."

His breathing is becoming more labored.

"Maybe you should rest a bit," I say.

He takes a moment.

"Did you enjoy my story?" he asks.

"Yes, I did."

"Good, because you need to get good at sharing yours. It helps people."

I arch an eyebrow.

"Don't end up like me – broke and broken. Make better choices. Let the world know what you are capable of."

I ponder his advice.

"Thank you," I say. "That was very kind of you. I'm so sorry things have to end this way for you."

"What's important is that they don't have to end this way for you," He says. "It's too late for me, and, yes, there are actually moments in life when it is too late." He's straining to speak. "Young people think old people are useless, and maybe some of us are. But we have life experiences that can help you to make better choices. Help you to avoid the same mistakes. But it's up to you to listen. It's up to you to choose."

The ambulance comes to an abrupt halt and a door slams.

"Thank you, Mr. Jones," I say. "I am so moved that you would share your story with me. It means a lot to me."

"I know they sent me home to die," he repeats with saddened tone. "And you seem like a nice kid," says Mr. Jones. "I like nice kids."

The doors to the back of the cab open wide.

"C'mon, old man. It's time to take you home."

SEVENTEEN

February 11, 1989 – 9:35 AM

"God. What a day," I lift the coffee mug to my lips.

We're at the station, sitting at the dinette table, engaging in small talk.

"You ain't kiddin'." Trevor glances at the newspaper. "I wonder if the cat made it."

I throw him a puzzled look.

"Just curious," he adds.

"My daughter's number three in her graduating class," Joe announces against the backdrop of *Emergency!*

Nobody gives a shit.

"Number three out of two hundred and fifty-nine graduating students," he adds.

"What time did you guys get in last night?" Dennis shouts across the room.

"About five thirty this morning," Trevor says. "We stopped for breakfast after we dropped off the old man."

I open my mouth wide, take in a lung full of air and exhale. "Man, I'm tired." I raise my arms and stretch. "What'd we get, four hours of sleep?"

Trevor checks his watch. "Yeah. About that."

"That ought to get you through the rest of your shift." Dennis laughs. He knows we're not getting out of here until six tomorrow morning.

"Doesn't anybody care that my daughter is graduating third in her class?"

"No!" shouts Mark.

"You're just jealous." Joe pours himself a cup of coffee. "I'm buying her a car for her graduation present."

Joe seats himself at the table.

"You know she's graduating this May." He takes a drink of coffee. "Gonna take her shopping for her graduation dress. Buy her one for the prom too."

"Why doesn't her mother take her shopping?" Trevor comments.

"You know her mother left us when Amanda was just nine years old. It's been me and her ever since."

Trevor shakes his head. "So that's why he hates women," he says with a hushed tone.

I nod.

"How are you able to buy her a new car?" I ask.

"I didn't say new. Gonna buy her a 1949

refurbished Ford custom coupe. Forest green. Classy."

Trevor and I trade glances.

"Got it all picked out already," Joe says.

"Just wondering how you do it, Joe, while the rest of us struggle with the little amount of money we make."

"You don't, Jimmy. I never hear you complain about your paycheck."

"That's because I don't have a family to provide for and I don't have many bills."

"Well, count your blessings."

Whoort! Whoort!

"Channel Two. EMS assignment. Gunshot wound. One Four Four Twelve North Forty-First Street. West Valley." Joe runs to the phone. "Station Eleven."

"Units Seventeen and Twenty-Four. Code three," Joe shouts.

"Shit. That's my place," Dennis says with a tone of concern.

*****

February 11, 1989 – 10:12 AM

A squad car blocks the entrance to the alley. Blue and red lights flicker on top the roof of a white Chevy Impala. A gold stripe borders the top of a thick band of blue that runs along the side of the four-door sedan. The word Police is printed in white on the two front doors, the golden emblem of the Phoenix on the back. It pulls away from the entrance. We guide the ambulance in.

Several police officers walk the scene.

There's a man. I can't see his face. Light yellow hair, cut military style. About five foot eight, I'm guessing. Stocky. He's surrounded by four police officers. Two hold him face down to the side of the squad car while the other two spread his legs and cuff him.

We stop the ambulance and get out. Dennis and Mark are right behind us. Firefighters arrive. There are four of them. They get out of their vehicle and join us.

"Hey, Jimmy."

"Hey, Rick." I nod to acknowledge the other three.

Police officers pull the man away from the squad car. One of them opens the back door. They turn the man around. His gaze meets mine.

They guide him into the back seat, dunk his head under the roof. The door slams shut. His face visible through the window.

I stare at him, throwing a silent question.

"You're not gonna believe this."

"What?" Trevor asks.

"Look." I nod toward the squad car.

A shocked expression takes hold. Trevor pauses a beat. "Holy shit. That's Anderson."

"Yeah."

We walk over to the police officer who is standing beside a squad car, talking with another officer. "Hey, Bret. Tim."

"Jimmy." They cast a look down.

"What happened?" I ask.

Bret points to the red Buick Century. "He shot her in the head."

"Anderson?"

"Yeah."

"We'll go ahead and check it out," says Rick.

"Shot who in the head," Dennis asks.

"His wife," says the police officer.

"Mary Beth?" Dennis says, his voice wobbling.

"I'm sorry, Dennis," says the police officer. He gazes deep into Dennis' eyes. "I'm so sorry."

Dennis runs to the passenger side of the Buick. We follow. Firefighters are working to pull her out of the car.

"Let me see her," Dennis says.

I peer into the interior of the vehicle. It's drenched in blood. Brain matter spattered throughout. A .357 magnum lies at the center of the bench seat, where a console might have been.

I walk over to Dennis. I stare in horror.

She's covered in blood. Her dark brown hair tangled in the sticky red mess of brain matter. Pieces of skull, blasted away.

Dennis' face drains of color. Tears prick his eyes. He stares in dumb terror.

I want to do something. I don't know what to

do. My mind's in a schizophrenic state. I search through conversations with Mary. There's nothing there.

"Let's get her on the tarp," one of the firefighters says.

They place her body on a large piece of blue tarp that had been lain out on the ground. They fold it over her, enveloping her.

Tim calls the funeral home. "We need a First Call vehicle, stat."

Dennis and I turn to walk away. He releases a primal roar.

"Dennis," I try to divert his attention.

He turns a circle. I can tell he's in a rage. His face is red with anger.

He draws the attention of the police.

"Take it easy, Denny," says Bret. "We're all in shock."

"But she was like a sister to me."

"I know."

Dennis' face twists with sorrow. He clenches his fist. Draws his knuckles to his mouth. Bites.

How do I calm him? What should I say? Guy just lost a loved one, and I don't know what to do!

He glares with feral eyes at the squad car. Anderson flicks his gaze down.

Dennis lunges. The police hold him back. He screams, "What'd you do to her, you fuck! What'd you do?"

"Jimmy, get a handle on him," Bret says.

I take hold of Dennis' right arm, Trevor takes the left. Mark stands in front, "C'mon Denny. You can't let that sorry fuck do this to you."

"But he killed her. Murdered her in cold blood." Tears fill his eyes.

"I know," says Mark. "But you gotta calm down."

Dennis arches his head back. Lets out a silent scream.

The First Call vehicle arrives. The firefighters hoist the blue tarp into the back of the Suburban.

Tears glisten in Dennis' eyes.

He shrieks at Anderson, "You sick fuck!" Spittle flies. "We drank together. Partied together. Mary Beth was like family to me. So were you." He punches the air with his fist. Stomps his foot. "What kind of police officer puts a bullet in his wife's head?"

He's dizzy with rage.

"Let's get him outta here," Mark says.

I feel so helpless.

"C'mon, Dennis. Let the police handle this," Trevor says.

The First Call vehicle drives off.

We walk him toward the ambulance. He pushes back.

"C'mon, guy. Let's go. There's nothing you can do."

"I'm going to kill him," Dennis cries out. "I'm going to kill that mother fucker!"

"No, you're not," Mark says.

He glares at Mark. "Yes, I am. I'm going to kill him."

EIGHTEEN

February 12, 1989 – 2:17 PM

My day off. I walk over to the beige phone that's attached to the yellow wall in the kitchen. I lift the receiver, dial Mary's number.

"Hello?"

"Mary. It's Jimmy."

"Hey, Jimmy. I've been thinking about you."

"Yeah? What about?"

"Been wondering if any of that information I shared with you some time ago has been helpful."

"Yeah. I'm doing okay with it."

"You don't sound real convincing."

I twirl the telephone cord around my fingers.

"I'm kinda struggling with it. That's all."

"Explain, Jimmy."

"Well... when I can stay aware of myself and turn a potentially ugly situation around, I feel really good about it. Feels like I'm making a difference..."

"And you are," Mary cuts in.

"Yeah. But then, I have my moments."

Mary draws out a, "Y-e-e-s-s?"

I run my fingers through my hair.

"Moments when I behave as if we've never had the conversation, like I have no knowledge or recollection of any communication on the subject matter at all."

"So you stumble now and then."

"Not acceptable to me."

"Don't you think the expectation you set for yourself is a little high, Jimmy? I mean, do you really expect to run out the gate with this stuff and be a hundred percent spot on every time?"

"No, but I do expect to hold myself to a higher standard of care and not to do stupid shit and say hurtful things that the patient is going to remember."

"What in the world are you talking about, Jimmy?"

I press the receiver close to my ear. "The patient I kept calling a fat ass."

"Oh..."

I tell her about the six hundred pound woman. Explain how we set ourselves up for a quick trip to the hospital. Told her how I responded when I realized we would be spending a good portion of the evening trying to save her life. Then went on to describe how the patient reacted when I told her it was me that kept calling her a fat ass. How she cried. How I had hurt her.

"I'm sorry, Jimmy."

"Yeah. Me, too. Very unprofessional." I exhale a heavy stream of air. "And then when we went to clean the ambulance, it was very clear to me how badly we treated her."

"Did it bother you?"

"Yeah. It bothered me. Trevor basically told me to blow it off. So I did."

"Rough," Mary says.

"I'm so disappointed in myself."

"Jimmy." Mary commands. "Don't you think you're being a little hard on yourself?"

"Why?"

"Because you can't change a lifetime of programming overnight."

"Yeah, I know," I say, my voice trailing.

"It's difficult work, and it's even more difficult when you haven't gone through the therapy."

"Yeah," I say with a flat tone.

"You gotta think about the end result, Jimmy. What it is you want to achieve."

"Which is...?"

"I don't know, Jimmy. You tell me."

A long pause.

"I want to be kinder to people. I don't know why I can't be kinder to people. And I want to be the example others will follow."

"You gotta work at it, Jimmy. There's no other

way around it. And if you want it that bad, you'll accomplish it one day. You just gotta do the journey, learn to love the suck of it."

"The suck of it," I repeat. I run the picture of what that looks like in my mind. "A good way to put it."

"You should do the therapy."

"Ah, Mary," I say with a tone of annoyance in my voice.

"What?"

I snort.

"Did you hear about Anderson?"

"No. What's he up to?"

"Shot Mary Beth in the head with a .357 Magnum."

Mary lets a short surprised intake of breath escape over the phone.

"What happened?" she asks.

I briefly describe the scene of the murder – how Dennis was on the call – how we had to drag him off the scene.

"Dennis? On the call?"

"Yeah." A pause. "You should have seen him. God, I wanted so bad to calm him, but I couldn't find anything in our conversation that I could apply to the situation."

"Oh, my God…. And they were like family to each other. Didn't Dennis and Mary Beth grow up together?"

"Yeah, from like when they were infants."

"Man, I just can't imagine." She skips a beat. "Anderson's a police officer for crying out loud. Someone we rely on to protect us, not gun us down."

"I would have never pegged him for something like this either. Christ, they all three hung out together at Kelly's ever since Mary Beth married Jack. Heck. They practically lived together they were so close. The thing that gets me is what could she have done that was so bad?"

"I don't know, Jimmy. You know them better than I do."

"I just can't imagine what she could have done that would justify a bullet to the head. And it's not like I can ask Jack, either. And if anybody knows, nobody's talkin'."

"I'm sorry, Jimmy."

"I feel sorry for Dennis. The last words out of his mouth were that he was going to kill Anderson. To look at him, you'd think he meant it." I exhale a heavy sigh. "I just wish I could have done something."

"Terrible," Mary says. I imagine her shaking her head.

"What are you gonna do? I find myself saying this a lot with our guys. 'Wish I could help.' 'Wish I knew what to do.' Guess I should just accept the fact that this is part of the job. Just isn't anything anybody can do when we're faced with trauma we can't handle. It doesn't happen all the time, but happens often enough. Too often."

"Maybe you should look into becoming a Crisis Response Specialist."

"A Crisis Response Specialist? What do they do?"

"They're people who are trained to help employees and employers deal with catastrophic events."

"How so?"

"They get the subject to talk about the trauma. I don't know a whole lot about it, but, as I understand it, they probe the subject with questions."

"What kinds of questions?"

"I'm not exactly sure. I know they get the subjects to describe in their own words their experience of the trauma. Then I think they go on to ask things like, how did it make them feel, why did they feel that way, what did they see, anything that gets them talking about it so they don't internalize the effect the traumatic event has on them. Make sense?"

"Yeah. Kinda," I say.

"I'm hearing of great results from this kind of work. You should look into it."

"Maybe I will," I say.

Mary inhales a deep breath.

"Look, Jimmy. I just want you to know that you're doing a good thing. It's important to care about people. We don't do that anymore. I really admire what you are doing."

"Yeah?"
"You do care about people, right?"
"I do."
"Then, you're going to be okay."

NINETEEN

Trevor and I stroll into the station. We clock a glance around.

Sitting in the kitchenette, Mark strums his fingers on the table, his gaze pinned to an episode of *Emergency!*

"Where's everybody at?" I ask.

"Out on calls," Mark says.

We pour ourselves a cup of coffee. Take a seat at the table.

"Reading some good quality material, I see."

"Fuck you, Jimmy," Joe says, thumbing through the swimsuit issue of a *Sports Illustrated* magazine.

Dennis lifts a glance. "Hey, Jimmy. Trevor." He raises a mug for a sip of coffee.

I place my coffee cup on the table. "How are you

doing, Dennis?"

"Oh. He's doing just fine, aren'tcha, Denny?" Joe cuts in – his gaze fixed on the magazine.

"Yeah. I'm doing okay."

His expression morphs into sadness, then back to stolid. He reads his newspaper.

I lean back in the chair, rub my thumb over the handle of my cup. A ray of light casts shadows against motes of dust that flicker in the air.

I eye Dennis. "If you need anything…"

"Quit babying him." Joe interrupts. "All this compassion shit makes a man weak, right, Dennis?"

Dennis shrugs indifference. "If you say so."

"What do you think, Mark?" I ask.

"Huh – uh. I ain't that stupid." Mark rises from his seat and moves to the sofa that's located in front of the TV.

Joe turns a page. Studies the magazine. "She's just another dead broad, that's all."

"God. You're cold," Trevor says shaking his head. He folds his arms, leans back in the chair.

Dennis lifts a wry look. "She's not just some dead broad, Joe. She was like a sister to me."

"Yeah. Well, she wasn't your sister, and she got her brains blown out." Joe turns a cold shoulder. Flips another page.

"Why would you say something like that, Joe?" Dennis says, his face twisted. "You trying to make me feel better? Cuz if you are, it ain't workin'."

Joe waves a dismissive hand. "What's the use."

Trevor and I trade glances with Dennis. "No. C'mon, Joe. What's your point?" Trevor says.

Joe glowers at Trevor. "My point is, they're all the same."

"Who's all the same?" I ask.

"Broads. Broads are all the same. Here. Look at this one." He holds up the magazine. Points to a beautiful blonde who is scantily clad in a very tiny bikini. "I don't care who they are or where they come from. They're good for one thing and we all know what that is."

"And what is that?" I ask, his cavalier attitude working its way under my skin.

Whoort! Whoort! Whoort! Whoort!

"Channel Two. EMS assignment. Sports injury. Thunderbird High School. Seventeenth and Thunderbird Roads. Central Phoenix. Engine Twelve."

Trevor answers the phone. "Station Eleven."

We wait a beat. "Ambulance Twenty-four. Code three."

Dennis rises from his chair. Mark joins him. The call is theirs. They take their time.

"I'll be back," Trevor says as he rises from his seat, leaving his coffee cup behind.

I sit up straight, hug my cup with both hands. I turn to Joe.

"What the hell are you doing?" I say with a gritting tone. "Couldn't you have treated Dennis

171

with a little more respect?"

"He got respect."

"How? By belittling someone he cared about?" I say with astonishment.

"Look, Jimmy. He needs to learn to handle the facts."

"What facts?" My throat tightens.

"She was probably screwing around on him."

"What gives you that idea?"

"Why else would Anderson shoot her in the head? The way I see it, he just removed another headache." He winks. Casts a sardonic grin. "No pun intended."

A fury boils up from within.

"You're an idiot, you know that?" I yell.

"Fuck you, Jimmy."

"Fuck you! What if it were your daughter we were talking about? How would you feel then?"

"Well, it ain't my daughter we're talking about, now is it?" he sneers.

I blow out a snort of derision.

"Besides, I raised my daughter decent. She knows not to fuck around on her husband when she gets married."

"Right. Like you have any control over that." I move in closer, gripping my cup tighter. I pin his eyes. "All this business about Mary Beth running around on her husband, it's pure speculation. You haven't a shred of evidence to justify that any of it."

"Ah, c'mon, Jimmy. What else could it be?" His

tone takes on a seductive quality. "They all do it, ya know."

"No, they don't, Joe. Mary Beth is not your ex-wife."

"Right." Joe picks up his magazine with a dismissive air.

I glare at him for a long pause.

"Jesus, Joe. It's attitudes like yours that make it difficult to treat people with kindness."

"It's attitudes like yours that make it easy for people like me to run circles around ya'll."

I pause several beats. Take a sip of coffee. Place the mug on the table.

"You're a disgrace to the human race. You know that?"

"Eat your heart out, Jimmy."

Whoort! Whoort! Whoort! Whoort!

"Channel Two. EMS assignment. Rollover. The interstate at Higley. East Valley. Engine Twelve."

I rise. Run to the phone. Lift the receiver. "Station Eleven," I answer with a hard edge.

I pause a beat, "Copy." Slam the receiver into the cradle.

"Trevor!" I yell with a clipped tone.

"Yeah."

"We're up."

TWENTY

February 23, 1989 – 4:55 PM

"Fucking bastard!" I yell as I pull the ambulance out of the station. I flip the switch for lights and sirens.

"You can't let him get under your skin, Jimmy. You should see yourself."

"What."

"Your face is beet red and your eyes are bulging. Looks like you're about to have a stroke."

"Yeah? I'm so pissed at that bastard I could bite nails." I exhale a grunt. "You didn't hear him, did you."

"No. What'd he say?"

"That idiot assumes that Mary Beth was screwing around on Jack and is all but celebrating her death." My tone carries an edge that makes it clear that I just want to beat the living fuck out of him. "And I should just ignore that?" I yell.

Trevor's face knots. "I guess not." His gaze strays to the side window.

"Worse yet. How do you make life a little happier, a little easier for people when assholes like that show up in your space." It's more of a statement than it is a question. "Like a stick in a fan," I add with a snort.

"Jimmy. I don't know why you're even going down that road."

"What road?"

"The one where you want people to be happier or some shit."

"Yeah. Me neither. But it's something I want to do."

My mind churns with thoughts as the anger subsides.

"There's got to be a way."

"A way for what, Jimmy?"

"A way to deal with assholes like Joe."

"Why you wasting your time?"

"Because."

"Because why?"

"Because life is worth it."

Trevor lets out a heavy sigh.

Buildings fly as I press my foot on the pedal. I round a corner. "If I could just find a word, a something that I could revert to when I find myself in situations where I struggle."

I flick my thumbnail off my teeth.

"I just have to remember not to participate in

the problem. I'm having such a hard time not participating in the problem."

"I wish I could help you, Jimmy, but you know my head ain't anywhere near that pool of water."

"Just need to master treating people unconditionally," I say absently.

"What do you mean, unconditionally?"

"You know. Just accepting people and situations for what they are, without judging and without trying to control the outcome. Remembering to not participate in the problem. That shit."

"Is that what you mean by unconditional?"

"Yeah." I make a left-hand turn.

"Well, Jimmy. I think you have your word."

I work the ambulance through traffic that is being rerouted off the freeway. Arteries are jammed. I scan for access.

"What word?"

"Unconditional," Trevor says.

I take a left over the freeway pass.

"Where you going, Jimmy?"

"Gonna get on the freeway from the off ramp."

"You're kidding. You're gonna get us killed."

"Do you see another way?"

Trevor clocks a glance around.

"Shit. No." Trevor instinctively stiffens his body, bracing himself for impact.

"Unconditional, huh?" I say, feeling around the word. "I like that."

"I thought you might."

"Why didn't I think of it?"

"You're too much in the thick of it," Trevor says.

"I hate it when I don't connect my dots."

I guide the ambulance slowly onto the off ramp against oncoming traffic. Vehicles move to their right to let us by. Others slam on their brakes to ward off an oncoming collision. I eye expressions wrought with question.

"This is crazy, Jimmy."

"Turn on the radio."

We inch our way down the off ramp. A siren sounds from behind. A quick glance into the rear-view mirror reveals red and blue strobe lights.

I knit my brows. "What the fuck?"

"It's the police, Jimmy. What are you going do?"

I exhale a long hard breath.

"I'm gonna keep driving."

*****

February 23, 1989 – 8:07 PM

We approach the scene.

A moving truck with black lettering idles at an angle, crossing two lanes of freeway. A police motorcycle has skidded to its side, resting underneath the truck. A smattering of debris extends across the open road.

A swarm of deputies, dressed in dark brown polyester slacks and tan short-sleeved button down shirts, cordon off the area, leading traffic away from the scene. Their hardened expressions reveal the sorrow that comes naturally when a fellow officer has been seriously injured. It's as close to home as losing a loved one.

I spot the injured officer. He lies about twenty yards from the truck.

I brake. Doors open. Red and blue lights are on my tail. We get out of the cab and run to the back to pull our equipment. I am greeted by a clean-shaven, square-jawed deputy with a military style haircut and cold black eyes.

"Officer?" I say.

"You're under arrest."

His partner joins him. Young. Scrawny kid with a dimple in his chin. Stands there like a useless auto part.

"What for?" I ask with grated tone.

"For evading the police and endangering the lives of others."

"Seriously?" I breathe out a fretful sigh. "You've got a fellow officer lying in the middle of the freeway in critical condition who seriously needs our help and you're going to arrest me?"

Trevor stands beside me, mouth agape, his expression a complete question.

The deputy casts a glance to the one sprawled on the freeway.

He pins my gaze. "Okay. Go."

We lift our equipment. Head toward the fallen

officer.

"What the fuck is that all about?" Trevor asks.

"Hell. I don't know. Some deputy with an ego the size of Mount Rushmore deciding to be high and mighty today," I say.

I eye a young man with tan skin and a muscular build leaning against the noise barrier. His forehead is plastered into the palm of his hands and his left foot is perched on the wall behind him. Another young man of similar build stands to his side.

We run to the fallen officer. He's unconscious. Firemen are working frantically to intubate him. Paramedics dress the wound on his crushed chest. Others take his pulse, secure the IV, ready him for transport. They work in sync with a coordinated skill set resembling that of clockwork.

Trevor throws the airbag to the ground. We drop to our knees. Fellow officers hover, while another officer paces. They watch our every move.

I eye the twisted compound tib fib fracture with the bone jutting out of the boot. The shaft of the black boot tops the officer's knee.

"He's losing quite a bit of blood," Trevor says. "I'm gonna cut the shaft so we can dress the wound."

"No!" Shouts the officer who suddenly stops pacing.

Trevor's gaze flicks up to the short, husky offender with a thin mustache on pock marked skin. "Whaddya mean, no? We gotta stop the bleeding."

Trevor and I scan the leg. The tibia has punctured the skin, impaling the shaft of the boot, so that it protrudes into space like a baseball bat that's been shoved through a chain link fence.

"We've got to cut the boot to dress the fracture. Not only is loss of blood an issue, but we risk the development of osteomyelitis, as well," Trevor adds.

"What the fuck is osteomyelitis?"

"Inflammation of the bone that's usually caused by bacteria."

Pinching his chin, the officer pauses. I can see he's running the information through his mind.

He furrows his brow. "No. You're not cutting the boot."

Trevor cranes his neck, scans the glum expressions of other officers looking for support. None given.

He tosses a glance to the ground. His face twists.

"It's all right, Trevor. We'll find another way."

Trevor lifts a look. "You really care more about that boot than you do his life?"

The officer dismisses Trevor with a wave of his thick hand.

That pisses me off.

Trevor's gaze meets mine.

"You know," I say to the officer. "I'm really working hard here to be kinder, more compassionate, but it's really hard to do when we're being dismissed as nonessential. You should have a little more respect."

The officer glares at me and repeats, "You're not cutting the boot."

"I'll make sure to share that with family members if the officer dies," I say.

"You lookin' for trouble?" the officer threatens.

"No. We just need to cut the boot."

"You're not cutting the boot," he reiterates with feral tone.

Trevor shakes his head with disgust.

"What assholes," I say under my breath.

I reach into the airbag to pull supplies.

"What are you doing?" The tall lanky police officer with a comb over asks in a curt tone.

Trevor glares at him. Snorts.

An anger boils up. Mary's words pound in my head. *Don't become part of the problem.*

I catch his eye. "We have to stop the bleeding and since you won't let us cut the boot, we're going to have to fill it with gauze and tie a tourniquet around his leg."

He eyes us with suspicion.

"Okay. Go ahead," the officer allows. "What's that rubber band thing for?"

"It's the tourniquet," I supply.

Trevor and I work. The officers watch. We stuff the boot with gauze, working to dress the leg from inside as best as we can. I apply the tourniquet. We splint his leg. Paramedics bring the backboard. Trevor and I finish up. They load the patient onto the backboard, secure him, and carry him away.

We gather our supplies. Rise to walk away.

"What is it with these guys who think they are better than us?" I say. "Aren't we all working to accomplish the same thing? Save somebody's ass?"

"I don't get it either, Jimmy."

"Really pisses me off. No respect."

We arrive at the ambulance. Open the doors. Throw the equipment inside.

There's a tap on my shoulder. I turn around.

"I'm putting you under arrest."

I exhale an exasperated stream of air. "Really?"

"Really. You broke the law. Put the public in danger. What you did back there could have resulted in a serious situation."

I shift my weight to the other foot.

"It was the only way I could get onto the freeway."

"Let it go, Ray." I dart a sideways glance. It's the officer who wouldn't let us cut the boot. "Just let it go."

They trade glances. The arresting officer takes on a sullen expression.

His cold, heartless eyes peer into mine. He turns and walks away.

"Sorry about that," says the officer who saved me. "He sometimes gets carried away with himself."

I feel my expression change to a question.

"Thank you," I say.

I pause a beat.

"About that little tiff back there," I say. "I was out of line. I'm sorry."

He lifts his gaze. "Forget it."

I dart a glance toward the freeway.

"How are the other officers taking it?" I say.

"As well as can be expected, I guess." He lowers his head. Hooks his thumbs into his belt.

"I'm sorry for your loss," I say.

The officer nods appreciation. "You boys headed out?"

I peer into eyes revealing spasms of pain. "Yeah. Our work is done."

The officer casts a glance toward the ground. "Well, I got work to do."

"I know."

He lumbers toward his fellow officers, shoulders rounded, head slumped. He carries the weight of his pain in his stride.

"Wish I could do something to make him feel better," I say to Trevor.

Trevor meets my gaze. Shrugs his shoulders.

TWENTY-ONE

March 22, 1989 – 1:23 PM

We're stationed at a local apartment complex today. Kind of unusual, but it happens from time to time. It's warm outside. Hot, actually, about eighty-five degrees which is high for this time of year. Been that way for the last few of days. Eighty-two degrees one day. Eighty-three degrees the next. We decided to take advantage of the rare opportunity to bathe in the sun during the last week and a half in March, when normally, it is still fairly chilly.

We're poolside. The air is still. Skies are clear. We're in our swim trunks, and the sun bears down on our bodies with ruthless tenure.

"You're burning, Trevor."

"Yeah. I know," he says. "Never could take the sun."

"Here. Put some suntan lotion on."

I toss him a dark brown plastic bottle with a

picture of a little girl whose puppy is tugging at her bikini bottom.

The radio cuts into the stillness. A/C D/C, White Snake, Twisted Sister – the music wafts over glistening bodies nestled comfortably in lounge chairs.

"I'm hungry," declares Al.

"Burgers are almost done." Steve flips a couple of burgers, pats them with the spatula, then rolls the dogs. "Hot dogs are ready if you want one."

"I'll wait."

The u-shaped two-story complex shields the pool from public view. Rolling green grass and scattered palm trees lend a tropical feel to the environment. The black scanner, with its cord plugged into a socket on the wall, sits on the table of the outdoor bar that is decorated with colorful Mexican tile.

"Man, I'm cookin'," Frank says as he rises from his lounge chair. His driving privileges have been restored and he's back to work. "I think I'll take a quick dip."

"Water's awfully cold," Dennis warns.

"How cold?" A look of concern crosses his face.

"About sixty, sixty-five degrees," Dennis says.

Frank pinches his lower lip.

"Go ahead Frank," Mark encourages. "You'll only feel it for a minute."

Frank hesitates. He eyes Mark who takes a drink of soda.

"You're from Minnesota, Frankie. Sixty degrees should be warm to you," Al calls out.

Frank's body is silken with sweat.

"Go on, Frankie. You look like you could use it," Trevor says.

Frank gives a quick glance. Without hesitation, he runs across the deck, jumps into the air. He grasps his knees, pulls them under his chin. Seconds later – a huge splash. Water sprays up as Frank plunges, then surfaces again, shaking the water from his face. He swims to the deck, pulls himself out of the pool and collects a long blue beach towel to dry off. "Invigorating!" he laughs.

Dennis shakes his head.

"The temperature's perfect," Frank says while drying his hair with the towel.

"Yeah, right," Dennis chuckles.

"Seriously. You should take a dip."

"Uh-huh. Do I have 'Stupid' written across my forehead?" Dennis replies.

"Burgers are ready!" shouts Steve.

"So glad Joe is off today," I say to Trevor.

"I hear ya, bud."

A violent intrusion. Our surroundings quake. Stricken with surprise, we become silent, but for the music.

A rainfall of shattering glass follows. It collides with the groan of screeching metal – a protest to the violation of its own substance in the most egregious of ways. An explosion of debris bursts forth crashing to the earth and is followed by a loud thump. A car alarm sounds.

"What the hell was that?" Trevor says.

We clock a probing glance at each other, each with a look of clueless wonderment in our expressions.

"Sounds like it could be a good car accident," I say to Trevor. "Turn up the scanner, Steve."

I shoot a glance at the pool fence to make sure our uniforms are handy and conjure up thoughts of what those sounds could possibly translate into. I rise from the lounge chair, my body gleaming with sweat. I throw a glance to the pool. It's *so* inviting. *Don't do it, Jimmy.* I quickly weigh the pros and cons. *I got a quick minute.* I jump in then immediately climb out, shaking the water from my head. I shiver, take hold of a beach towel and walk to the bar where the scanner is located. I take a seat and wait.

Whooorrt! Whooorrt!

There it is.

"Channel Two. EMS assignment. Auto accident with injuries. Fifty-Ninth Street and Rose."

"That's across the street," Steve says.

"Seventeen and Twenty-Two. Code three," the scanner adds.

"Frank. Take over the barbecue, will ya?" Steve yells.

"Let's go, Trevor. I think this is going to be a

good one," I say, aware of the excitement in my tone.

We change into our uniforms and race to our ambulances. It seems a bit ridiculous to drive across the street, but we need our equipment. Steve and Al climb into their ambulance. We exit our ambulance from the complex. We enter a haze of dust and floating particles. The murky substance obscures our view.

Trevor slows the ambulance. I open the door and jump out before the ambulance brakes.

The air is thick. A sickening pall of gasoline and oil makes breathing difficult. Broken parts of metal, tires, a fan blade, a battery, the radiator, hoses, a panorama of unidentifiable debris, indiscriminately strewn across the landscape. I eye the mutilated car pitched beside a downed palm tree in the middle of a grassy field. The hood is smashed in kind of a rounded out U-shape and shoved into the body of the car. The body of the car scrunched into the rear. The white picket fence completely annihilated. An impression of a crumpled ball of paper flashes to my mind. Except this one is metal.

I run to the ball of metal, dodging debris along the way. I toss a glance to the two bodies that are trapped inside. I eye the one who is pinned between the engine and what used to be the driver's seat of the car. His blood-spattered face is smudged with blotches of oily dirt. Lacerations cut deep into his forehead. His eyes closed, head slumped, black hair covered in dark red blood. His head is crushed in. His chest moves up and down, like he's breathing, but he isn't. This guy is dead. It's taking a minute for the brain to receive the message.

A hand moves so very slightly. A light stream of air releases a whisper of *help*. I crane my neck to view the body trapped in a metal casing of where I assume the passenger's side used to be. He hangs midair, held by a metal piece that managed to wrap itself around the victim, holding him in.

I drop to my knees. Dumbstruck with terror. I study his round face. Arteries of blood spill onto his cheeks. Near his eyes. Around his nose. Rust-colored blotches of mud vie for attention among lacerations – some deep, some interspersed with oily patches of filth. Sandy brown hair is caked in rich red blood. His head supported by something. I have no clue what it is. An arm dangles over the metal casing, the other trapped beside his body. His legs are pinned. He's around my age and he's alive.

Trevor brings the equipment. Steve and Al are right behind.

Sirens sound in the distance.

Trevor throws the air bag to the ground. "Whadda we got?"

"Two trapped bodies," I say.

Steve and Al join me to evaluate the situation. "We need a hurst tool," Steve says casting a worried glance Trevor's way.

Trevor throws a look around. "Shit. Where's the

damn fire department when you need 'em?" He exhales a heavy breath.

"This guy's dead." Al indicates the body pinned by the engine.

"What about the other one?" asks Trevor.

"He's alive," I say.

Trevor eyes me.

The victim releases another weak breath of '*elp*.

I take hold of his hand. He must be suffering horribly. Or does the brain shut down when the body encounters such a violent assault?

"Hold tight," I say. "Help is coming."

I scrutinize his face, isolating the particles that make up the smudge. My gaze bears down into the genetics.

"Jimmy."

I flick a look to Trevor. "Yeah."

"You okay?"

"Yeah."

My attention rivets back to the victim. An uneasiness percolates within. *What's that word?* An uncomfortable uneasy feeling. *Unconditional. I've got to be unconditional.* I eye his hand. Concentrate on his hand. *I've got to hold his hand.*

Firefighters arrive. Five men, dressed in black protective gear, descend the monstrous fire truck.

"We need a hurst tool!" shouts Al.

I study his eyes. They're closed. *Peel 'em back.* I hesitate. Then peel the lid back. *Green. His eyes are green.* A wave of panic. A childhood memory. My heart thuds – the rush of blood pounding my ears. My breathing quickens.

"Jimmy."

Trevor's voice.

"Do you want some gloves?"

I eye my hands. They're covered with blood. "No."

I move my gaze to his face. Examine the blood, how it pools around the eyes, trails onto his cheek, the dark red, sweet sticky copper-smelling ore that is becoming one with his features.

Firefighters arrive with a small orange generator and something that looks like an oddly shaped pair of scissors encased in a cylinder like body. A firefighter starts the generator. Its powerful motor roars. The hurst tool is connected. Firefighters operate the scissors with the dexterity of a seamstress. They cut into the metal. It roars back a rebellion as if to reflect a pain from the throbbing assault. I imagine a terror that screams from the attack.

"Hurts," he barely whispers.

I snap my attention back to the victim.

"It's going to be all right," I say, cupping his hand into mine. "Everything's going to be just fine."

A dreadful foreboding looms.

I eye his mouth. His dry lips quiver slightly as his body jerks with the movement of metal. I stare with deadpan terror as fear crawls through me, inching its way through every fiber of my body.

The roar of the generator ratchets up another decibel. Scissors clash. Metal snaps. My victim drops. I catch him in my arms, scan for Trevor. He works the legs to free the man. We place him on a backboard. Begin c-spine immobilization procedures.

I feel Trevor staring at me.

The police arrive. Two vehicles flashing blue and red lights. The officers exit and walk the scene.

"I've got a 901 H here!" Trevor yells over the roar of the generator.

"Let's get a tarp on the ground," someone shouts.

Steve and Al intubate the patient.

I hold his hand. Blend into his expression. Tears prick my eyes.

"Jimmy, you all right?" Trevor asks, his gaze throwing the question.

I gaze at Trevor.

"Yeah. Why?"

"That look on your face – like you've just seen a ghost."

"I don't know why." My voice wobbles slightly.

Trevor arches a questioning eyebrow.

"I'm good," I supply.

"Okay. Then take his vitals or something, will ya?"

"Oh. Sure."

Trevor prepares the IV.

I'm lost. I feel so lost. Off balance. Seized with

uncertainty. As though I'm in a *Twilight Zone* series where time stands still, the earth is eviscerated, and I'm alone, not knowing what to do for the next step.

I stare at the patient. Fear and anxiety pump through me like two powerful locomotives. A wrecking ball sits in the pit of my stomach.

"Here, Jimmy. Let me help," says Al, glancing at me with a look of concern.

Al and Steve work on vitals.

I cup the patient's hand in mine. "Hang on," I say softly. "We're doing everything we can."

Trevor eyes me again.

We load the backboard into the ambulance. I climb in. Sit beside the patient. Take his hand. I'm focused on his presence, willing him to live.

"I'm gonna ride in the back with you, Jimmy."

"Yeah, sure."

"Al, can you drive?" Trevor asks.

Al climbs into the driver's side. We close the doors to the patient's cabin. Steve steps into the other ambulance, starts the engine, and drives away.

Trevor continues checking vitals. I make sure I'm holding the patient's hand, and wonder why the need is strong.

Al slots the key. He shifts the gear into drive, presses on the gas pedal.

"Look," Trevor says indicating the windows on the doors.

193

I peer through the window as the ambulance pulls away, eyeing the vehicle that has effectively been dissected by the jaws of life. The scene disappears as I view the police rolling the dead body – the 901 H – into the blue tarp.

The First Call vehicle arrives.

Firefighters disperse.

A shivering dread runs up my spine.

I glance at my patient.

A sadness sweeps over me. I feel a desire to cry.

*****

March 22, 1989 – 3:38 PM

We arrive at the hospital. Ambulance doors swing open. The medical team moves quickly to transfer the patient and continue resuscitation efforts. I stand back and watch.

Within seconds, the medical team disburses. The patient is moved off the floor.

Mary is walking toward me.

I feel heavy. So very heavy. Like a waterlogged sponge.

"He didn't make it," Mary says.

Tears well.

"Are you okay, Jimmy?"

She probes my face, searchingly.

"Jimmy. You look like your mother just died."

"I'm fine."

"I don't think so, Jimmy. Your expression is

telling me something very different."

I dart a questioning glance.

"Like you're not really here with us right now. Your eyes are distant and not focused," she adds.

I shrug indifference.

"I'm gonna have Trevor take you to see Sam."

"Who's Sam?"

"Sam's a Critical Incident Stress Debriefer."

"I'm fine. I don't need to see anybody."

Mary examines my expression.

"Yeah. I can see that," Mary says with a bit of a sarcastic edge. "I'm calling Sam."

TWENTY-TWO

March 22, 1989 – 5:25 PM

Tension strums through my body as I wait in Sam's office. I feel like a pregnant cloud drenched in moisture – floating through the motions yet hindered by a heaviness I can't explain. He's with me – that man – the one whose hand I held all the way to the hospital. He's pasted like a photograph on the wall of my mind.

"Jim?"

"Yeah."

"I'm Sam Cummings." His voice is calm, a deep baritone that I find soothing. He extends a hand. I take it and shake.

"Have a seat." He points to the love seat at the opposite end of the room. He takes a chair. Runs his fingers along the pencil that rests in the crevice above his ear.

"Would you like some water?"

"Sure."

He rolls the chair over to the mini fridge that sits on the floor to the left of his desk.

I eye the older man who is somewhere in his fifties, salt and pepper hair cut close to his scalp. A mustache of the same color covers his full upper lip. Large blue eyes emanate kindness, or maybe its compassion. I'm not sure. His silver wire-rimmed glasses seem to accentuate the size of his eyes, making them appear larger than they really are. His large frame fills the black mid-century, tufted executive chair that sits on a base of industrial casters, making it easy for him to swivel and roll. He pulls two bottles of water from the fridge.

I'm seated on a black love seat, patterned after his. It's positioned between two barrel-shaped club chairs of the same color. I eye the certificate of achievement that hangs on the wall. The paper is old and yellowed. It's framed with a faded dark brown wood that looks like it has not been serviced in a hundred years. The remaining walls are barren. Papers are piled high on a gray metal desk that's butted against a dingy white wall. The room is small – almost claustrophobic.

He hands me the bottle of water. "Mary called to let me know you were coming."

"I'm not sure why I'm here." I place the water at my feet. "I told her I was fine."

He opens his bottle, takes a drink, closes it up,

and sets it on his desk.

He exhales, probes my expression.

"I see. Do you know what we do here?"

"No."

I mate my fingers. Rest my forearms on my thighs.

"We specialize in crisis intervention, working with people who have been exposed to acute adversity, trauma, or disaster. Basically, we assist individuals in crisis."

"What's that got to do with me?"

"Sometimes, we don't realize how badly an event may have affected us."

I rub my temples. "I told Mary I was fine."

He leans back into his chair, clasps his hands behind his head.

"You want to tell me what happened?"

I pause to run the scene through my mind.

"Nothing really. I went on a call like I always do. Handled it like I always do."

Liar.

Sam sits up, places his elbow onto his desk, leans his cheek into the palm of his hand.

"Tell me about it."

"Just a couple of kids in a car accident. That's all."

"Did they get out of the car and walk away? Or was it something a little more serious?"

"A little more serious."

"How serious, Jim. Give me some details."

"You can call me Jimmy."

"Ok, Jimmy. Tell me about the car accident. Describe the scene. How badly was the car hit?"

"It wasn't the car that was hit. It was a palm tree."

I glance at Sam looking for a reaction. There is none. No feelings of emotion. No hint of impatience. He's calm, his countenance, peaceful, like he had just been blessed by Jesus Christ himself.

I relax a bit. Visualize the lump of metal in my mind.

"It was a white something. No way could I guess the model of the vehicle. It was so smashed up that I don't think anyone would have ever guessed it was once a car. It looked like someone took a metal ball and threw it onto the field."

I reach for the bottle of water.

"The car had to be traveling a hundred miles or more an hour to completely sever that palm tree the way it did. It was a good-sized tree, too. Hit the ground with a thud that shook the grounds."

"Did the kids eject?" Sam asks.

"No. They were inside the vehicle."

"*Inside* the vehicle?"

"Yeah."

I told Sam about the one who was dead, how his chest cavity rose up and down, and how it reminded me of a bicycle pumping air. Then I told him about the other – the one who was still alive – and how I was sure he was dead. I told Sam of the cry for help and how it rattled me.

"Why?" Sam asks.

"I couldn't imagine anyone surviving that crash. I imagine he must have been in terrible pain."

"Probably so," Sam says.

"I couldn't believe this man was alive."

"Man? I thought you said they were kids."

"I don't know why I keep calling them kids. The man was about my age. Both of them were."

"Interesting," Sam says rubbing his chin.

"What?"

"The way you refer to the men as kids." Sam throws a glance to the ceiling. "Okay. Maybe we'll come back to that later." He leans forward. "Please continue. What were your thoughts about him being alive?"

"I don't think I had any. I was so taken back by this, what...? miracle...? that my mind froze."

"Why do you think that happened?"

"I don't know. All I know is I witnessed pain, agony, terror, confusion – they all seemed to come together into one great big..." I pause. "I don't know. All I know is it shook me. There was something familiar about it."

"Familiar? Expand on that a bit."

"I wish I could, but I can't put a finger to it. Just an uncomfortable sense of familiarity."

"Interesting." Sam rubs his chin again. "Tell me what happened next."

I told Sam how I wanted to make the man feel better, how I took his blood soaked hand into mine. How I didn't bother to put on any gloves. I spoke of studying the face, scrutinizing the features. Examining him to the point of nearly neglecting his care.

I sink deep into the memory, like I'm in the movie that's playing in my mind.

"There was a sense of familiarity gnawing at me, like I knew him. But I didn't. Yet the familiarity plagued me – like a disease."

Tears well, rising unbidden. I take off my eyeglasses. Place them on the love seat beside me.

"Then something tells me to check his eyes. So I pull back the eyelid."

Tears spill. My breathing catches.

"What do you see?" asks Sam.

The image – so vivid.

"What do you see, Jimmy?"

I cup my face, remembering every detail of the man whose hand I am holding.

"It's me!" I sob in terror. "It's me!"

"It's you?"

"Yes. No. I don't know. He looks like me."

My shoulders quake.

The moment seems to require a long silence.

I continue to weep.

Sam hands me tissues. I sniff back tears. Blow my nose.

"I kept asking myself, 'What if that was me?

What if this was me?' and each time I asked the question, fear would take a stronger hold of me."

I dab at my eyes.

"Why did you think that was you, Jimmy?"

I lift a look of confusion. "I don't know. It's just, looking at him, I was seeing..."

My jaw clenches.

The flash of memory resurges. A shiver sweeps through me.

"What is it, Jimmy?"

"It's nothing."

"Had to have been something. Your expression changed pretty noticeably."

"A childhood memory, that's all," I say dismissively.

"Interesting it would pop up now. Tell me about it."

I eye Sam, reticent to share the memory.

"Please tell me about it," Sam says.

His peaceful demeanor encourages me.

I hesitate. Sam waits me out. I feel his power emanating.

"When I was a kid I had something happen to me."

I take a drink of water to take the edge off. I've never shared this story before.

"At the time, I didn't think anything of it. Looking back, I realize the danger I put myself in."

I place the bottle on the floor.

"I was somewhere around six or seven years

old. I made a friend in school and I wanted to play with him. My aunt, who was watching over me at the time, didn't have a way to take me there. There was no bus service, and the friend's mother didn't want to come and get me and made it clear she wouldn't drive me home. I finally convinced my aunt to let me walk, but her approval came with a warning. 'Be back by dark or I'll tell your father, and you know he'll beat you with the belt if you're not back.' I promised I'd be back."

It feels like I have cotton in my mouth. I swipe the bottle of water. Chug a gulp or two. I mate my fingers. Rest my forearms on my thighs.

"The friend lived a long way away. It was taking forever to get there, and it felt as if the sun would go down before I arrived. I was determined to have play time with my friend, so we played until the sun had nearly crested the foothills. That's when I realized I wasn't going to make it home in time."

I clench my mated hands tight and bring them up to my chin.

"I left my friend's house in a hurry. His mother was true to her word. She wouldn't drive me home. So I walked. Panic set in as it got darker, and I began to run. Panting like spent kids do, I had to stop. I was afraid, horribly afraid of what my daddy was going to do to me. My daddy was mean when we were kids, and he'd take no mercy with using that belt. I knew it." I breathe heavily through my nose. Sam waits patiently.

"I got this bright idea to hitchhike. I saw other people do it. It was pretty common back then. I put out my thumb. It only took a couple of minutes. A man in a pickup truck stopped for me. I climbed into the passenger side and shut the door. I told him where to take me, but he didn't do it. He was driving 'round and 'round to no particular destination, just driving, and he put his free hand on my thigh up under the leg of my shorts. I was pushing his hand away, yelling at him to let me out of the truck. He wouldn't do it. All I could think about was my daddy beating me with that belt. I was waterlogged in fear, but it was misdirected, focused on my daddy's beating. Remembering how much that hurt. Not having a clue as to what this man might have had in store for me."

I shiver.

Sam watches me.

"What happened after that?"

"I just kept screaming 'my daddy's going to beat me if I'm not home by dark.' I screamed it over and over again. 'Let me out of the truck!' He kept driving. He wouldn't stop. He kept putting his hand up under the leg of my shorts. The darkness was creeping in. My panic grew more intense. I started to cry. Then suddenly, out of nowhere, he stopped the truck and let me out."

Tears prick my eyes. I blink. Electrical impulses course through my veins, like tiny needles prickling my skin.

"That's probably what saved you."

"What?"

"Your sole focus on getting home and avoiding that beating."

I nod acknowledgment.

I heave a dry heave.

I hold my stomach. I heave again. My eyes water.

"You okay?" Sam asks.

"I don't know." The heaving subsides. "I think so."

I'm drained. I lean back into the love seat.

"Did you make it home on time?" Sam asks.

"Yes."

"How did you feel?"

"Relieved." I snort a chuckle.

A sinking feeling suddenly hits me.

"I never thought anything of what that man was doing until I got older and learned about pedophiles and what they do to children."

I chew on my lower lip.

"How close I came to a living terror that I might have had to live with the rest of my life, or worse yet, a terror that could have easily ended in my death."

I lay my head on the back of the love seat. I inhale a deep breath. Tears stream down my cheeks.

"It haunts me to this day."

TWENTY-THREE

March 27, 1989 – 2:20 PM

The phone rings. I lift the receiver.

"Hey, Jimmy. It's Mary."

"Mary. I'm so glad you called."

"Oh, good." I sense a sigh of relief. "Then it's safe to assume your meeting with Sam went well?"

I turn my back to the kitchen wall and lean, looping the telephone cord through my fingers.

"It was phenomenal, Mary. Really productive."

"Do you mind sharing with me?"

"Not at all."

I tell Mary about the man in the truck and how Sam helped me to discover the link between the experience of my childhood, the encounter with the accident victim, and the ensuing fear it produced. I talk about the physical reaction I had to the memory, how the heaviness left me, how I felt drained and vulnerable afterwards – but in a good way. I explain how Sam said it would take a few days or so for the experience to fully process through me – something about my neuronets rewiring and that when I was complete, I would feel a renewed sense of stability.

"And do you?" Mary asks. "Feel a renewed sense of stability?" she adds.

"I do."

"I knew you'd like him," Mary says.

I mention to Mary that Sam gave me his card, told me to keep him posted on my progress, and even invited me to come back to see him again.

"I was so moved by his caring, his kindness. I mean he genuinely cared," I add.

"Yeah. Sam's a good man."

"Makes a difference when someone actually genuinely cares. He had such a profound impact on me that I'm thinking about taking a class to become a Critical Incident Stress Debriefer."

"Really."

"Yeah. I think so. Gonna talk to Sam about it. Get a little more information. See what it would take to move forward."

"Sam's a good one to talk to about that sort of thing. I'd encourage it."

"Thanks."

"By the way, I think you'd make a great debriefer, Jimmy."

"Why's that?"

207

"I just know you."

"Yeah, well."

Ice cubes clink. A gulp follows.

"Hey, Mary. Thanks for all you do. I really appreciate it."

"You deserve the best, Jimmy. Don't ever let anybody tell you otherwise."

I feel my face crimson.

"Hey. Guess what?" I say.

"What?"

"You know how I've been challenged with not participating in a problem?"

"Yeah?"

"Well, Trevor helped me come up with a word that's going to handle that."

"Really. What word is that?"

"Unconditional."

A pause.

"Great word. How's it going to help?" Mary asks.

I note the reticence in her tone.

"I figure unconditional means to accept people for who they are. Not judge them, right? Let the situation play itself out as it is, without me trying to direct the outcome or insert my own need to be right."

"Y-e-a-h," she stretches the word.

"So when I find that urge to become part of the problem, all I have to do is think the word unconditional, and it will help me to remember to keep the emotion out of it. To remember that it is about them and not about me, right? To accept the person or the situation as it is?"

"Yeah," she says, stretching the word again.

I sense a drifting of her presence.

"Mary?"

"Yeah."

"You with me?"

"Yeah, Jimmy."

"What's going on?"

"God, Jimmy. You said something that's really resonating with me."

"What's that?"

"Our need to be right. That's really what these arguments and infractions are all about, isn't it? Our need to be right?"

"Uh. I don't know."

"If we could just let that go – let the need to be right go – wouldn't the world be a better place?"

I pause to let that sink in.

"When you put it that way." I think a minute. "And now that I'm considering it, it does seem to me that my level of participation is motivated by how strong my need to be right is. Wow. Interesting."

"Mm-hmm."

"Now, if only I can make unconditional work for me and let go of my need to be right. Maybe be-tween those two, I can get a better handle on my reaction – catch myself before I become part of the problem."

"Maybe, Jimmy. As long as you remember that unconditional doesn't mean you let people walk all over you. Don't let them cross your boundaries. You can care about people and let them be right without having them step over your boundaries."

"What do you mean step over my boundaries."

"Best way to sum that up is not to let them disrespect you."

"Oh. I get it."

"It's about self-esteem and self-respect and being the bigger or better person."

"I get your point, Mary. I'm going to work on this."

Mary gulps. A muffled sound lets me know she's placed the container on a padded surface.

"Well, we got a lot of the world's problems solved today with just two words." Mary chuckles. "Unconditional and caring."

My mind receives the two words as though stakes have been driven into the flesh of my brain. A thudding sensation pulses through me.

"Important words," I say.

"I believe they are, Jimmy. There's a lot to learn and you'll have a lot of great stories to tell."

"Great stories to tell?" I rub my eyes.

"Yeah."

"What *is* this with great stories to tell?"

"What are you talking about, Jimmy?"

"I had a G.I. bleed who once told me the same

thing. Told me I needed to get good at telling my stories like it was important. I blew him off, but now I'm hearing it again."

"It helps people."

"How so?"

"It just does. Let's them know they're not alone."

"Hmmmm."

"Life is a story in motion, and like any other form of entertainment, some of it good, lots of it not so good. I've heard it said that we are in charge of our lives, that we can create our own stories. I don't really believe that. I'm more of the notion that we've been dealt a hand of cards. We might be able to choose the game, but more than likely, the game has chosen us. We're the one who gets to play, and it's how we play the game that determines our stories. Play well, my friend. Share your stories. It's like teaching others how to play their game. It's one true way to live forever."

I pause briefly, pinching my lip.

"Maybe if I put it in writing..."

"Then do it."

TWENTY-FOUR

March 31, 1989 – 4:13 PM

Homes of luxury pass by as I press my foot on the pedal. Trevor and I are in awe of the large sprawling structures that edge the street as though vying to be voted the most beautiful on display. Pride emanates from these Paradise Valley homes, and a vision of puffing chests putting their best foot forward pops into my mind. The road is freshly paved. Lush green landscapes provide ample space between properties. A generous population of shade trees and other ornamental shrubs lend a cool feel to the neighborhood. Wealth pulses through this small segment of the valley like the blood that pulses through my veins.

I take a right into the circular drive that leads out to the street on the other side of the yard. A police car is parked under the carport that shades the double wide mahogany doors. The drive is narrow and we can't get through. We park behind the police car.

This home is a little less pretentious. Set back a distance from the road, the sandy-colored structure seems dwarfed compared to its neighbors. Palm trees of various sizes and shapes line the circular drive. A weeping willow and an African sumac interrupts the flow. Tall bushes of rich green shrubbery align with plants of sage and golden bamboo to obstruct the view of the glass block picture window that winds its way westward toward the back of the house. A three car garage is located on the east side, attached to the building in its circular design. Small spatterings of deer grass and other ornamental shrubberies populate the gravelly landscape that butts up to the road. A mail box is perched front and center where it borders the street. There's a quaint feel to the panoramic view. Trevor and I exit the ambulance, take our gear, and scurry through the open doorway.

"Officer." I nod, acknowledging the tall policeman with a sunken chest and a delicate frame who is standing in the foyer. His small shoulders make him appear to be extra thin and lean.

He returns the nod, lifting an arm to point us in the direction of the patient.

Sounds echo off cathedral ceilings as we pad down the hallway. Elaborate sculptures line tops of what looks like cherry wood cabinetry. The walls display large and small colorful pictures – artwork that looks as if it costs a fortune.

We enter the room. A stocky, middle-aged man lies at the center of his four-poster bed – unconscious – suffering from agonal respiration. His eyelids flutter with rapid eye movement.

Firefighters arrive. Rick's about five feet eight, black hair styled in a classic taper look. Veins trail the bulging biceps – a clear indication that he pumps iron. His narrow hips reveal his level of fitness. Randy exhibits the same. His hair is auburn, eyes brown. Same style of hair cut. They're both strong. They help us move the patient to the edge of the king-sized bed. The patient feels extra warm to me. I place my hand on his forehead.

"Let's get him intubated," Rick says.

I remove my hand. "He's really hot."

My comment is met with silence. Trevor and Rick prepare for intubation. Randy readies the IV equipment.

Using his left hand to steady the patient's head, Rick opens the mouth to insert the oral airway. He guides the tube into the lungs. "Wow. You're right, Jimmy." They finish the intubation and secure the bag valve mask. Rick pats the patient's face and arms, holding steady long enough to feel the density of the heat. He furrows his brow. "It's like he just came out of the oven."

I pull the thermometer out of the airbag. Take the patient's temperature.

Trevor retrieves the penlight. Checks the pupils in the patient's eyes. "Man. You're right. He *is* hot."

Randy inserts the IV needle.

Rick locates the cardiac monitor. Delivers it to Trevor.

Trevor attaches the leads to the patient's chest. Rick turns some dials, flips the switch. The monitor beeps. Red and blue lights flicker.

I read the thermometer.

"A hundred and eight degrees!" I provide incredulously. "Nobody's a hundred and eight degrees!"

I check his pulse.

"I can't get a decent count," I announce.

Rick, Randy, and Trevor study the monitor with questioning expressions. The squiggly lines are performing abnormally.

"Man, his heart rate is all over the place," Randy says.

Rick gives a hard look. "You ain't kiddn'."

"His pulse is inconsistent. It's changing rapidly," I supply.

"Yeah. That's what the monitor shows." Trevor blinks.

"Something's really weird about this," I say. "I'm going to check around the house. See if there's anything that might give us a clue. You guys got this?"

"Yeah, go ahead," Rick nods.

I hasten to the master bathroom. Survey the

room. On the right, stands a walk-in shower tiled in white porcelain, laced with gray marbling and encased in seamless glass. A claw-foot bathtub, big enough for two, faces a picture window the size of the wall. It showcases a swimming pool centered in the professionally landscaped yard of rich green trees, colorful flower shrubs, and lush green grass – all designed to make one feel as though he is in paradise. I walk over to the custom-made cabinets with dual sinks.

I scan for a clue – anything unusual. The countertops are clean. I open the drawers and rummage through the contents. Aspirin, Tylenol, lotions, aftershave, bobby pins. Clean.

I rush through the bedroom passing Rick, Randy, and Trevor, their gazes pinned to the cardiac monitor. Trevor moves the chest piece of a stethoscope around the victim.

I walk the hallway. Enter the guest bathroom. It's decorated with simple accoutrements. Knick knacks of two fairies border folded towels that are shelved under the sink. A candle sits in a glass container that hangs on the wall. Granite countertops are bare except for the soap dispenser. I pull at the mirror on the wall. It doesn't open. I pull at the brown cabinet drawers. They roll out easily. I rummage through the contents. Nothing.

I exit the room. Run down the hall. I spot a doorway. I glance inside. Looks like a spare bedroom. I clock a glance around. *No evidence anyone's been in here.*

I circle down the hall. Spot the study. I step inside. Cast a glance to the shelving units lined with books from floor to ceiling. The color matches that of the mahogany executive desk that centers the room. A small hand-painted Victorian floral lamp sits on the edge. A calendar, pencil holder, and calculator balance out the landscape. Pictures of family are scattered around. I open the drawers and shuffle through the contents. Nothing.

I raise a look to the shelving units. Chew my lower lip.

I can't help myself.

I walk over to examine the books. I scan the authors, running my fingers along the base. Freud, Machiavelli, Tolstoy, Dostoyevsky, Aristotle, Jung – all authors a friend of mine encouraged me to read. It's been so long ago.

The familiarity weighs on me. I pause a beat to remember who made the suggestion. The memory eludes me. I shake my head slightly.

I enter the hallway to complete my round. It dumps me into the other side of the foyer where we first arrived.

The tall police officer who initially greeted us is joined by a hard-body, athletic type who looks like Daniel Craig – the actor who starred in the James Bond series. The athletic one is taking testimony from one of the neighbors. The tall one is holding a small crowd at bay to preserve the scene.

"Officer," I call out to the tall one.

He tosses a look my way.

"Can I have a word with you?" I ask.

The officer steps away to join me.

"What's up?" he asks, looping his thumbs into his belt.

"I'm not sure. Just wanted to ask if you had seen anything unusual."

"Like what?"

"I don't know. Evidence of any kind of questionable activity," I respond.

He clocks a glance around. "No. I haven't seen anything out of the ordinary for something like this."

I stare into disinterested eyes.

"No drugs or any evidence of that nature?" I ask.

"No."

"Any idea at all as to what might have happened?"

"None. The neighbor over there called in saying she found him lying on the bed unconscious. I guess she noticed the front door had been opened and wanted to make sure everything was okay." He waits a beat. "Why do you ask?"

"Patient's got some weird symptoms. Symptoms my partner and I haven't seen before. Was wondering if maybe there might have been some kind of foul play involved."

"None that we could identify."

Trevor bursts into the foyer.

"Jimmy! We gotta get him to the hospital stat. He's diminishing quickly."

I nod acknowledgment.

"Thanks, guys," I say to the officers with a wave of my hand as I depart.

We return to the bedroom. The cardiac monitor behaves like its malfunctioning. It startles me. I check the patient's temperature as we ready him for transport.

"His body temperature is increasing," I say with alarm. "What in the world could he have taken to cause himself to bake?"

"I dunno, Jimmy."

"It's like he's cooking from the inside out," I add.

With Rick and Randy's help, we slide the body onto the gurney and secure the patient.

We run the gurney to the back of the ambulance and load him in. I join the patient. Trevor turns the engine. Firefighters depart. I check the patient's vitals. Trevor backs out of the circular drive. He's headed straight to St. Rita's.

TWENTY-FIVE

April 11, 1989 – 8:59 PM
Another night. Another call. Another opportunity to practice my new attitude.

Gunning the ambulance, I barrel down well-lit streets toward my destination. Trevor turns on the radio. Lyrics from Pink Floyd's *Wish You Were Here* blast in the cab. I round a corner. Take a residential street. Gun the engine to speeds of fifty and sixty miles per hour. The darkened road makes it tough to see. I'm focused on the pavement in front of me. The glow of headlights lead the way.

A flash of yellow eyes slam hard into the windshield. The body bounces off the rooftop.

I brake. Tires screech against the asphalt.

"What are you doing, Jimmy?"

"Gonna save the cat."

"What?" His tone incredulous. "We gotta save

the man who's down. Remember that call?"

"Give me a minute. I'll be quick."

I open the door, get out of the cab. I eye the yellow mix breed that lies dead in the middle of the street. I mourn the dead cat. Move it to the side of the road.

"C'mon, Jimmy!"

I climb back into the cab. Shift the gear into drive.

"You and those fucking cats."

"Well, they're people too," I defend. "Besides, I just can't imagine how the family will feel when they learn I killed their cat."

"You gonna tell them?"

"Yeah."

*****

April 11, 1989 – 9:27 PM

He's sitting on the sidewalk – slouched against a building. Legs outstretched. Right hand at the flank under his left arm. Left hand holding his right elbow in place. He's caked in layers of filth and just as many layers of clothing. Years of dirt alter the color of his skin. Bright blue eyes peer out amid grime petrified in the folds of his emaciated face. His hair is wild and stiff. He hasn't shaved, ever, I'm sure, and his filthy black beard hangs down to his chest.

We eye the victim then exchange glances.

"Just another homeless guy with nowhere to go," Trevor observes. I nod agreement.

We step out of the cab. Approach the victim.

I blow out a heavy stream of air. "Jesus!" My eyes water. I turn a one-eighty. "This mother fucker stinks!" I say to Trevor.

Trevor eyes the listless man.

"Holy Christ, dude! You ever take a bath? Maybe think to use a toilet?" Trevor gags. "Get up and get into the ambulance."

The man struggles, rolling to his knees, using his hands and feet to push himself off the cement. He stumbles. Folds his way to the ambulance. "My side." He winces.

"Jimmy, get the door. Make him sit in the jump seat. I ain't cleaning up after him."

I do as I'm told. "Get in."

The homeless man crawls up the step, veers toward the gurney.

"No. Not there," I shout. "There." I indicate the jump seat behind the driver's side of the vehicle. I retch.

He hoists himself into the seat.

Trevor starts the engine.

I stare at the hulk of stench sitting opposite me. He sways.

Mother fucker's drunk.

I watch him as we ride to the hospital, snorting out heavy breaths through my nose, trying to get the smell out.

I wonder if I should check his vitals or something.

I retch again.

Huh- uh. No. Not touching that.

Thoughts churn as Trevor guides the ambulance.

What about being unconditional?

I consider my commitment.

Sorry. No can do.

I take a beat. Revisit my commitment.

Nope. Not this one. I ain't sullying our equipment on someone who doesn't really need treatment, especially when they smell this bad.

He slumps over sideways. I push on his left side to keep him from falling. My hands sink into something wet, sticky.

I grimace. Push him against the wall. Make sure he stays put. I pull my hands back. They're soaked in blood.

"Shit."

I drag the homeless man off the jump seat and lead him to the gurney. I extract a pair of scissors from the metal supply cabinet. Cut through the blood-soaked clothing. The acrid odor hits me like a fist to the face. It's unbearable. I step back. Exhale a hard stream of air. My eyes water again. I choke back vomit. Try to hold my breath while I examine the source of the bleed.

"Trevor. The guy's been stabbed."

"No way."

"Gotta get him to the hospital stat."

"Gotcha." Trevor flips the switch for lights and sirens.

I dress the wound then work the patient, checking vitals, inserting the IV needle, hooking up the oxygen mask. Trevor's drive takes on new meaning as I work.

We arrive at the hospital. The medical team takes over.

Minutes later.

"Trevor. You wanna give the report? I need to clean up."

"Sure."

I walk out of the washroom and join Trevor at the nurses' station. He finishes the report. We walk to the ambulance.

"I'm gonna toss the sheets into the dumpster. We'll never get 'em clean." Trevor agrees. "To tell the truth, I can't stand the thought of touching them," I add.

"Use your gloves, Jimmy. You seem to be forgetting to do that lately." I nod.

We remove the sheets. Wipe the equipment down with a strong disinfectant.

"Let's head back to the station," Trevor says.

"I want to stop and get the cat first."

"Really? You're kidding, right?"

"You know me better than that, Trevor."

*****

April 11, 1989 — 10:39 PM

I guide the ambulance slowly down Fifth Avenue, the residential street where I left the cat. Thoughts churn, and a flashback crosses my mind.

"You remember that cat we saved several months ago? The one we intubated and drove to the vet's office?"

"Yeah, I remember." Trevor casts a sideways glance.

"I wonder whatever happened to it."

My comment is met with silence.

"Do you know, Trevor?"

Trevor blinks. "Yeah."

I give him a curious look. "What happened to it?"

He shrugs a sheepish, "Mmm. I don't wanna tell ya."

"Why?"

"I just don't," Trevor says.

I pause a beat.

"The cat died, didn't it," I state sorrowfully.

Trevor catches my expression. Stares wide-eyed. He must have glimpsed a look of grief and disappointment. He gazes out the passenger window then casts a look to the floorboard.

"No, Jimmy. The cat didn't die."

"Well, then what happened to it?" I ask with an edge of irritation.

He gives a reticent look. Mumbles something.

"What?"

In low hushed tones he repeats, "I adopted it."

I slam on the brakes. Throw the gear into park. Pin Trevor's eyes. "You what?"

"I adopted it."

I exhale a long stream of air. Slap my knees. Snort a chuckle.

"You serious?"

"Yeah."

Then it hits me. The irony of it.

I press my lips. My stomach spasms. Spittle escapes. I can't hold it any longer. I guffaw.

"What's so funny?" Trevor crimsons.

He waits patiently.

"I don't see what you think is so funny," Trevor says.

I arch my head back. Laughing. Tears streaming.

Trevor clocks a look around. "Like you ain't never saved a cat before."

I choke back a breath. "Yeah, but you hate cats."

He chuckles. "I know. But this one was special."

The situation seems to require a long pause.

I catch his eye. A small chuckle. "What'd you name it?"

"Trauma."

I rub my chin. Smile. "Trauma. Good name."

"I thought so."

I wait a beat.

"Okay. Let's go find my cat."

Trevor arches an eyebrow. "You're really going to take the dead cat to the owner?"

"Yes, I am."

"Why?" Trevor says with puzzlement.

"I think they should know I killed their cat. They're probably looking for it."

"What makes you so sure."

"Because I would be looking for the cat if it was mine. Besides, I want to be a better person. Treat people better."

"That again?"

I glare at him for a beat. Then say, "Wouldn't you want to know if something happened to Trauma?"

"Yeah. But nobody would be stupid enough to track me down and let me know if something did happen to my cat."

Trevor eyes me. I'm certain he thinks I'm an idiot. I don't care.

"My point. So what's wrong with making a change?"

His gaze flicks down without a response.

"Can we go get the cat, now?"

He cocks his head. "Only if you promise not laugh at me anymore."

"I'll try. But you gotta admit it's pretty funny."

"Whatever." Trevor quips.

TWENTY-SIX

April 13, 1989 – 6:39 PM

It's early evening. I walk into the utility room at the station. Hang the keys on the rack.

"I'm goin' across the street. You want anything?" Trevor asks.

I picture the convenience store with two red stripes spanning the width of the stand-alone building. "Naw. I'm good."

" 'Kay."

Trevor leaves. I walk into the great room. Glance around.

No one here.

I lift a look to the rotary phone that hangs on the wall.

Good time to call Sam.

I snatch the receiver. Dial his number.

"Hello?"

"Sam. It's me. Jimmy."

"Hey, Jimmy. What's up?" he asks with a sing-song voice.

"I wanted to give a quick call to let you know how helpful your advice was to me." A pause. "Regarding the debriefing issue. I can't thank you enough for the conversation."

Footsteps.

"Glad I could be of help, Jimmy. Have you made a decision?"

Murmuring voices cut into the stillness. A jangle of keys hit a table.

"Yeah."

I glance up to find Mark with the remote control in hand and Dennis strolling to the kitchenette. "I'm taking a three-day course next week."

Mark presses a button. The TV flickers to life.

"Which classes?" Sam asks.

Mark places the remote next to the keys. Plops onto the sofa. Dennis joins him. Hands over a can of soda.

"Group Crisis Intervention and Assisting Individuals in Crisis. The ones you suggested."

A rustle of footsteps.

"You ever look at my daughter like that again..." Joe says with feral tone.

"Good, Jimmy. That'll get you certified once you pass the test," says Sam.

Sound bites from an episode of *Emergency!* puncture the room. I press the receiver tight to my

229

ear.

"I did nothing wrong!" Al shoots back. "Mandy's a kid. I'm not a freaking pedophile, Okay?"

"Tone it down!" shouts Mark.

"I know what I saw," Joe returns.

I place my hand over the mouthpiece. "Guys," I say with a sharp edge.

"What you saw was in your head. You're too damned protective of her. You imagine shit," Al rebuts.

"Hey guys. Can you hold it down a bit? I'm on the phone. Hold on, Sam. Mark. Turn down the TV, will ya? I can hardly hear the other end of the line."

They glower at me. Mark lifts the remote. Lowers the sound. The argument continues in softer tones.

"Sam?"

"Yeah, Jimmy."

"Where were we?"

"You're taking your classes next week."

"Oh, yeah. The ones that will get me certified.

"That's right. And I'd advise you to take the test as soon as possible while the information is fresh in your mind," Sam adds.

"I plan to. I saw where I could take advanced classes too. I might like to do that in the future," I say to Sam.

"That would be a wise thing to do. The more advanced training you get, the better debriefer you'll become."

"I'll give that some thought."

"Jimmy!" I dart a glance to Trevor who hurries toward me. A look of 'guess what?' sweeping his face.

I pull on the telephone cord. Turn to face the phone. "Look, Sam. I gotta run."

"Sure thing, Jimmy."

"I'm really looking forward to working with you," I say appreciatively.

"Me, too, Jimmy. Let me know when you've passed the test."

"Jimmy." Trevor's voice lilting to pique my interest.

"I will. Thanks again." I hang up.

"What," I say with clipped tone squaring off with Trevor.

"You know that guy we picked up in Paradise Valley a couple of weeks ago? The one that was really hot? And we couldn't figure out what was going on with him?"

"Yeah?"

"You'll never guess who it was."

We stroll toward the kitchenette.

"Who?"

"Doctor Hochman."

I stop. Throw a questioning glance. "Doctor Hochman? You sure?"

"Yeah, I'm sure."

"How do you know?"

"I ran into one of the nurses from the hospital."

"What's that about Hochman?" Dennis yells from across the room.

I pour a cup of coffee. "You want some?"

Trevor shakes his head. "He committed suicide."

"Suicide?" Dennis and I say simultaneously.

Dennis and Mark join us. We take a seat at the table.

"Hochman committed suicide?" Mark inquires with a questioning tone.

"Yeah," Says Trevor.

I pinch my chin.

"Why didn't I recognize him?" I say bleakly.

"I don't know, Jimmy. I didn't recognize him either." Trevor scoots his chair away from the table. Crosses his legs. Folds his hands behind his head.

"Why would Hochman want to commit suicide?" asks Mark, his face a question. He takes a sip of soda. Places the can on the table.

"Shit. I don't know," Trevor says. "Why does anybody want to take the coward's way out?"

"It takes a lot of courage to commit suicide," says Dennis glancing at Trevor.

I read a distant memory in Dennis' eyes.

"Why?" asks Trevor. "Did you ever try it?"

"I've seriously considered it a time or two," Dennis replies.

Trevor snorts. Lowers his arms.

"Things must have been pretty bad for him to take his own life," Mark says, drumming his fingers on the table.

"I can't believe I didn't recognize him," I say with somber tone. I take a drink of coffee.

"What does it matter, Jimmy. The bastard's dead," Joe cuts in. He pulls a chair. Straddles it to lean his arms on the back.

"You always this kind-hearted?" asks Trevor. Uncrosses his legs. Leans his forearms on the table.

"The guy committed suicide," Joe states flatly.

"That's right. Everybody's an asshole to you, right Joe?" Trevor says half in jest.

"Not everybody," Joe replies with arrogance. "My Mandy's perfect."

Leaning against the wall, Al huffs a derisive snort.

"And *you* keep your hands off of her," warns Joe.

"Fuck you," Al replies.

"Cut it out you two," I say. "Nobody's doing anything to your daughter, Joe. Give it a rest."

Joe gives me a hard look.

"Let it go, Joe," says Trevor.

Joe casts a glance to Trevor. Leers at him.

"Hey, Al. Would you get me a water outta the fridge?" asks Trevor.

"He was a good man," I say with measured tone. "A good friend of mine. And I didn't recognize him." A sorrowful feeling descends upon me. I feel a desire to weep.

Al hands Trevor a water.

My thoughts fill with the memory of the study. "He's the one who recommended I read those books," I add.

"What books, Jimmy?" Trevor takes a swig of water.

"I came across some books in his study. Books written by authors like Tolstoy, Machiavelli, Jung and others like them, and I couldn't remember who suggested I read them, until now. It was Hochman who encouraged me to read those authors." I lower my gaze to the table.

"So how'd he kill himself?" Joe cuts in, oblivious to the direction of the conversation. "Did he do something fun like put a bullet to his head?"

"You're sick, Joe. You know that?" says Trevor.

"You guys take life too seriously." He snorts sardonically. "Now, c'mon. Tell me. How'd he do it? Take a bunch of pills? Hang himself? Stab himself with a knife? What'd he do?"

Trevor and I trade glances. An expression of "idiot" firmly plants on Trevor's face. I'm thinking I'm mirroring that image.

"I'd like to know how he did it," says Mark sheepishly. "I'm kinda curious."

Trevor takes a swig of water. Places the bottle on the table. Pins Mark's eyes. "He shot himself up with insulin." Trevor blows out a stream of air.

"Oh. Cooked himself to death, did he?" Trevor darts a hard glance to Joe.

"Tasty." Joe winks.

"What a jerk," I say to Trevor with a hushed tone. I shake my head.

Channel Two. EMS assignment. Auto accident. Grand Avenue and McDowell. Engine Twelve.

The phone rings "Station Eleven."

A pause.

"Seventeen. Code three!" Mark shouts.

*****

April 13, 1989 – 7:57 PM

We're approaching the location where the accident was to have taken place. It's dark. A railroad track crosses the lonely four lane street lit with a street lamp. I guide the ambulance at a very slow pace. "Do you see anything, Trevor?"

He surveys the area. "Hunh-uh." He pauses a beat. "There's someone in that white Honda Accord over there by the barricades. Maybe they know something."

I pull up to the Honda parked under a street light that brightens that section of the road. I thrust my arm through the open window. Gently tap the side of my door.

A woman with long black hair and bright red lipstick peers out. She looks to be about forty-five years of age. Well-kept. "Can I help you?"

"I hope so," I say. "I'm looking for an accident that's supposed to have taken place around here somewhere. Did you happen to see anything?"

She opens the door. Steps out.

"This is it."

A mild shock hits me like I've walked into a clear glass door. "It is?"

"Yeah." Her tone is curt.

Trevor and I trade glances. We roll our eyes. Get out of the ambulance.

"My neck," she complains. "I can't move my neck." I eye the woman who's grasping her neck. She presses her lips. "I'm in excruciating pain," she adds.

"She'll never make it to the Oscars," Trevor whispers.

"What happened?" I ask the tall slender woman who is dressed in white slacks and a bronze colored button-down silk blouse. Her high heels match the color of her lips which strikes me a bit funny.

"The Camaro hit me from behind," she says. She points to the Camaro. "I was driving down the street and had to stop to keep from hitting the barricade, and he ran into me," she says with accusatory tone.

A bearded man dressed in khaki cargo shorts and a Hawaiian shirt leans against the Camaro. He's barrel-chested with a pot belly that hangs over the waist of his pants. He catches the woman's indication. He pushes off the Camaro and walks toward us. "I barely tapped her."

"I'll take a look at the Camaro," Trevor says.

"We weren't doing more than fifteen maybe

twenty miles per hour when she suddenly slams on her brakes," he continues. "I was casing out the area, you know, because of all the construction that's going on. I caught her out of my peripheral vision. Slammed on my brakes, but not in enough time to keep from nicking her. I mean I barely tapped her bumper. Check it out. There's no damage to either of our cars," he says with a crusty tone.

"My partner's checking out the vehicles now," I say. "Are you hurt?"

"Look at me. Do I look hurt to you?" the man responds.

I give him the once over.

Trevor pulls me to the side. "There's no damage to the Camaro. You find any on the Honda?"

"I haven't checked it yet."

"I'll check it out."

"My neck," the woman moans. "It hurts so bad. I can't move it." she repeats. I peer at eyes wincing as if in pain.

Trevor pulls me aside again. "She's faking it, Jimmy."

"I know. I'm going to treat her like a viable victim anyway."

"Why?" Trevor questions with a mocking tone.

"Because." I give him a look.

"Oh. That shit again?" Trevor huffs a "Jesus" and stomps away.

"My neck," she continues to whine as though we didn't believe her the first time. We didn't.

"Don't worry, Ma'am. We'll make sure you get the care you need," I say taking her hand.

She catches my eye. Probes searchingly. The tension in her expression eases. Her gaze softens. She weakens the hold on her neck. "Thank you," she says as though in shock.

The Hawaiian shirt crosses his arms. His face falls. His eyes narrow. Snorts an expression of disgust. Walks away.

The police arrive. Two aged men with balding heads and thick waistlines get out of the car. Guns strapped to their hips. A chattering radio laced over their shoulders. "Whadda we got?" an officer asks. The woman resumes her claim to pain.

I greet the firefighters. There are four of them. All about the same height and weight. Clean-shaven. Hair combed in the classic taper style. Bulging biceps under short-sleeved button-down shirts of navy blue. They could have passed for poster boys on the cover of a *Playgirl* magazine.

They clock a glance around the scene. Shake their heads. They've seen this before.

I feel about as useful as a garlic press. I walk the area. Note the barricades that bar entry into the intersection. Eye the two-foot trench that parallels both sides of a tract of land.

"They must be laying new track," I say to Trevor.

"Mmm-hmm," Trevor says with disinterest.

I eye the distance of the trenches that morph into darkness. The yellow caution tape runs visible for several hundred feet.

A distant buzz gently folds into the knots of subdued conversations.

"Let's go see if they need us any longer," I say to Trevor.

We walk over to the scene. The police and firemen are in conversation. The victims lean against their cars.

"Are we done here?" I ask the servicemen.

Muddled laughter bounces off the night and comingles with intermittent shouts of joy. The intensified buzzing draws our attention. I stare pointedly at the red moped heading straight for the ditch. Traveling at full speed, it carries two passengers.

"Hey!" I yell at the driver who is completely oblivious to the danger ahead. "Stop! You're headed straight for a ditch!" They disregard my warning. The police and firemen join me. "Stop! You're gonna get killed!" our shouts overlapping while we wave our arms and scream out caution.

The moped accelerates. The shrill of laughter pierces the night.

"Stupid, fucking kids!" a fireman shouts as he makes a quarter turn and throws his gaze to the ground.

"Stop! There's a ditch!" I shout again.

A loud thump.

The tires spin emitting a sound like a buzz saw that just cut through a core of wood.

The moped bites into the night sky tossing both bodies into the air – one to the left, the other to the right.

The police and firemen turn their backs – displaying an air of indifference. Expressions of the woman and the Hawaiian shirt show wariness of the situation.

"We need to get over there. Someone could be hurt," I announce.

My comment is met with disinterest. "You two," a policeman indicates the woman and the Hawaiian shirt. "You can leave now."

"Isn't anybody going to do anything?" I ask.

A policeman flicks a gaze at me. "Yeah. Sure." Returns to his notes while remaining in conversation.

"Stupid kids deserve what they got," one of the firemen murmurs.

"What if they're dead?" I ask.

They lift a lazy look. One arches an eyebrow. My question is met with silence.

"They could be hurt really bad, ya know," I add.

"Mmm-hmm," A fireman says. "Kids did something stupid and that's what stupidity gets you."

"Like you've never done anything stupid before," I say. "We gotta do something."

The servicemen glare at me with stoic

expressions. Makes me feel like I'm the stupid one.

I cast a bitter look. "Trevor, get our flashlights." I run to the back of the ambulance to collect our equipment.

"You serious?" One of the firemen says mockingly. "You really going over there to help those stupid asses?"

I glare at him. "Yes."

Flashlights crisscross as we run across the field. We approach the body. He's twisted. Unconscious. His blonde hair streaked with red. His face smudged with dirt. A gash over the eye. Looks like he's about nineteen years of age. Handsome little bloke.

I throw the airbag to the ground.

Trevor readies for intubation. I check for level of consciousness. Balling my hand into a fist, I place my knuckles on the boy's sternum and press with measured intensity. I remove my fist. "This guy's completely out. You ready to intubate?"

"Yeah."

I catch cylinders of light roaming the land out of the corner of my eye. I lift my gaze. Flashlights lead firemen and policemen lazily to the other victim.

We intubate our patient, clean his cuts, take his vitals, c-spine immobilize him, prepare him for transport.

"I'm going to run over and see if the other victim is ready for transport," I say to Trevor. "You wanna stay here with the boy? I'll be right back."

" 'Kay."

I run over to the firemen. The victim is standing, arguing with the policemen. "She ready for transport?"

"She's refusing treatment," a fireman responds. "Dazed a little bit but says she's fine. Just a few scrapes on her limbs from what I can see."

I eye her from a distance. Wearing blue jeans and a tee-shirt, she's about the same age as the boy. Her light brown hair tied behind her head in a ponytail. She's in heated argument with the police officer.

"The boy wasn't so lucky. I'm gonna go ahead and take him to the hospital."

"Suit yourself," shrugs the fireman. He walks away.

Thoughts churn as I run to the ambulance. So tempting to call him an asshole, but I'm not going to today. In a way, I can't blame him for his attitude. It is the problem I'm trying to correct. So I'll not participate. Not this time. I'll accept them for what they are. Accept the situation for what it is.

I'll choose to be unconditional.

TWENTY-SEVEN

April 26, 1989 – 5:50 AM

The door yawns. I step inside. Chatter from an early morning newscast cuts into the white noise of stillness that lingers in the room. I eye Roy sitting at the table in the kitchenette, his gaze glued to the newspaper. He blindly raises a cup, takes a sip, lowers it to the table.

"Roy," I say as I approach the classic white Formica table top brushed with stainless steel.

He glances my way. "Jimmy." His brown eyes glisten. "Thanks for filling in."

"Sure. No problem," I say to the man who bears a striking resemblance to Johnny Depp, the actor who stars in 21 Jump Street. "Trevor arrive yet?"

"No. Not yet. Help yourself to some coffee."

I nod a response. Place my materials on the table.

"What's up with your crew mates?" I ask as I pour myself a cup of coffee.

"Flu or some shit like that. Got several of them," Roy says without flicking an eye.

"Shame." I take a seat.

I clock a glance around. The TV screen on full display with a young male newscaster seated behind a desk, papers in hand, female to the side, prattling on about the news. A brown sofa faces the cheap entertainment center made of brown particle board that showcases the television and the black box purchased from Radio Shack. A black rotary phone hangs on the wall. Sleeping quarters hide behind closed doors, utility room off the kitchenette. Same set up as ours but in a much larger building. There's very little action here in rural Maricopa. And the irony of a larger space for fewer people strikes me as odd.

I take a sip of coffee. Place the cup on the table. Trail my forefinger around the rim.

"Where's Lisa?"

Roy raises the newspaper. Turns a page.

"Oh. She'll be here shortly. She's running late."

Very few females work in emergency medical services. Of the ones who do, most carry an air of masculinity about them, some with near the strength of a man. Lisa is of this lineage. She wears her dishwater blonde hair cropped short. Features – plain. Makeup never dares to see the light of day. She works out and it shows. She wears the uniform well.

The door creaks. I dart a glance in that direction.

I eye Trevor as he strolls to the kitchenette.

"Good morning, Trevor."

"Mornin'."

"Help yourself to some coffee," Roy says.

"Thanks." He drifts to the coffee pot. "Hey, Jimmy. How'd your class go?"

Roy lowers the paper. Cast a look my way. "What class?"

"I took some classes to become a Critical Incident Stress Debriefer."

"Yeah?" Roy says. "What's that all about?"

"I'm gonna help people deal with acute trauma."

"Good. We need something like that." Roy lifts his paper.

"So how'd it go?" Trevor repeats as he approaches the table. "You pass the test?"

"Yeah," I smile. "Gonna start working with Sam tomorrow."

Trevor pulls a chair. "And now that you're a Certified Critical Incident Stress Debriefer, no one will ever have a traumatic event again, right?" Trevor takes a sip of coffee. "Isn't that the way it works?" eyeing me, he chuckles.

"Yeah," Roy supplies. I think it's called Murphy's law or something like that."

I shake my head. Smile. "I'm going to refresh my memory. Study my stuff so I'm ready for Sam tomorrow."

"Good idea, Jimmy," says Roy. "Nothing ever happens in these parts anyway."

"Mind if I switch the channel?" asks Trevor.

"Naw. Go ahead," says Roy.

Trevor pads to the great room.

Roy lifts his paper.

I turn the pages of my manual.

Sound bites of *Emergency!* cut into the air.

*****

April 26, 1989 – 11:00 PM

"EMS assignment. Rollover accident. State trooper involvement. Route Three Eighty-Seven at Pinal Avenue."

The phone rings. Lisa answers. "Station Ten," her voice a strain of alto. She waits a beat. "Copy."

She slams the receiver.

"We're up," she announces. "All of us. Code three."

We snap up the keys from the utility room, head for our ambulances. I start the engine. Trevor flips the switch for lights and sirens. I pull out. Lisa and Roy follow.

"This oughta be a good one," I say to Trevor.

Trevor leans forward, pulls the zipper on his boots. "You're probably right. I just hope the trooper is okay."

"Yeah. Me, too."

I grip the wheel, speed down the highway, acutely aware of the pervading darkness that's encroaching upon us.

"Turn on the radio, wouldja Trevor?"

The knob clicks. He turns the dial. Forages through static.

Sirens blare. Their intensity seems to escalate the piercing sound to a whole new decibel level. Headlights pull the ambulance. Tires grind against the asphalt. Eyes pin to the road. I can feel the tension in my face as I search for evidence of the roll over.

Nothing comes through on the radio. A sudden turn of the knob annihilates the crackly noise.

"You okay, Jimmy?"

"Yeah. Just a little tough to see," I say. My voice strains.

Trevor leans back. Pulls a flashlight. Shines it into the darkness. The ambulance plows forward.

"How is it I got to be leader of this pack, anyway?" I say with edgy tone.

Trevor flicks his eyes up. Meets my question with silence.

I snort.

Keenly aware of my vulnerability to the darkness and the power it has over me, I heighten my senses. My belly tightens. I glance at the hands with a hard grip on the steering wheel. My knuckles have taken on a new shade of white.

"There!" Trevor yells, indicating the wreckage

on the road.

The ambulance brakes. Lisa and Roy brake to the right of us. We dismount. Strobe lights are enough to gather our gear. I collect a flashlight. Trevor and I hurry toward the wreckage. Flashlights crisscross against the corrosive void of darkness. I trip over something metal. Fall to my knees. The palms of my hands slam into the pavement. I manage to stay the flashlight. I rise. Rest on my haunches. Check the palms of my hands. Can't see them. "It's dark as fuck out here!" I yell.

"I'll turn on the headlights," Lisa shouts.

I feel for the flashlight. Point it to the errant object. A black bumper.

I rise from the ground. Chill at the all-consuming void of the night. I wait for additional lighting. I clock the flashlight around. "Where you at, Trevor?"

"Fuck if I know."

Lights.

Way better but not enough.

Flashing red and blues draw near. Three 5.0 Mustang LX Interceptors break. Six doors open. Headlights burn. We run. Cylinders of light beam from roaming flashlights – doing their best to guide the way.

We approach the black mass grounded in the center of the two lane highway. The vehicle is crushed as if a semi-truck had run over the top edges of it, the body heavily wrinkled, roof top sheared, the hood creased into the guts of the engine. An egregious assault to the pavement has the driver's side door crumpled into him. A wheel juts up and away from the wheel hub assembly – the bolts on which the wheels are normally mounted. The driver – pinned. The steering wheel jammed tight into his legs. There's no way this guy is alive. Heck. No one would ever guess this was once a 5.0 Mustang LX Interceptor – a Special Service Package designed specifically for law enforcement use.

I throw the air bag to the ground, kneel to the victim. Trevor, Roy, and Lisa hover. The troopers walk the scene. I glance through the opening where the windshield used to be. His eyes flick up to me. I lift a look. "He's alive."

I call for the helicopter.

Troopers rush to the wreckage. They pull at the Interceptor, heaving to upright the vehicle. Lisa and Roy find a spot to push. I join them. "It'd be so nice if we had access to a hurst tool and some light towers," I say before I exhale a heavy breath with a strong push.

"We're too far out for that kind of luxury," Roy supplies.

"Figures."

Grunts and moans dice the stillness. The vehicle releases a throaty resistance. I check the patient's status. He lifts a glance. "You okay, buddy?" I ask. He blinks.

We push and pull – the ten of us. More grunts. Heavy exhales. A swear word or several. This thing ain't budging.

"Trevor. Go get the rope out of the back of the ambulance and pull the ambulance up to the vehicle."

"Why? What are you going to do?"

"Gonna tie the rope to the car and use the ambulance to pull the body upright."

"Good thinking."

Lisa reaches through the windshield opening and places an oxygen mask over the victim's face. He winces. An officer reaches through to offer comfort. "Hang in there, bud." He falters.

Looking for evidence of expressions, I glance at the officers. I can't see their faces, just moving shadows – a consequence of the smattering of light derived from flashlights trained on the wreckage.

"Jimmy." Trevor hands me the rope. I loop it through the open windshield into the driver's side window and back around thinking to string it by way of the rear window. I hadn't noticed the window intact. An officer rushes to a squad car. Collects a tire iron. He returns. Smashes the rear window. We loop the rope through then bring it around to the front of the ambulance circling it into the windows at the front of the cab. We string it through the roof handle then tie it into a knot, pulling to make sure it holds. Trevor enters the ambulance, places the gear shift into reverse. He guns the engine. The rope pulls taut. Wreckage growls as though being seriously inconvenienced. We throw our weight into the carnage. Trevor accelerates. The taut rope strains. The screeching of metal violates the piercing stillness of the night. The vehicle tips with an aching groan. Trevor bears down on the pedal. The wreckage rises into a vertical swing, falling to its belly, sounding a boom that shatters the night.

Officers scramble. Three take to the steering wheel. The others work on the driver's side door. Trevor assists.

Roy works frantically to get the IV in place. Lisa's checking vitals. I check the victim's status. Eyes wide open. He's still alive.

The steering wheel defies the troopers' efforts. The officers grunt, baring teeth as they use every ounce of muscle to move the heinous vestige.

A distant sound of helicopters.

A baritone of metal cries wearily. The driver's door separates. The three men yank the door off its hinges then toss it. They join in the battle of the steering wheel.

A snap. The steering wheel inches up. I help. Push on the steering wheel. The victim's eyes catch mine. Another snap. The steering wheel flies. His legs are free. His eyes close. His face relaxes into an inanimate expression. I glare with alarm. "He's lost consciousness," I say out loud. I link my arms under his arm pits. Trevor works the legs. We gently remove the dead weight of his body and position it onto the backboard. I place my fingers on the carotid artery. Wait a beat. Move my fingers to the radial artery. "No pulse," I say. A shroud of sorrow engulfs me. My limbs seem to weaken. "Intubate him anyway." We c-spine immobilize him. Place him on the gurney.

Roy and Lisa intubate the patient. I clean up his cuts.

A thunderous roar of rotor blades crashes the night. I crane my neck. The helicopter has arrived.

We run the patient to the helicopter. Wind whips from the storm of the blades. Paramedics assist. We load him in. We know he's expired. They air lift him away.

Turning our backs, we stride to the small cabal that has formed near the headlights.

"That was a nasty roll," I say as we walk.

"Yup. He had to have been doing a hundred miles an hour or more to roll that many times," Trevor says.

"How many times do you think he rolled?" asks Lisa.

"A good ten anyway, dontcha think?" says Roy.

"Sure looks that way," I say.

"I wonder what caused him to roll like that," says Lisa.

"Probably a blowout. Or he hit something," Trevor provides.

We stride naturally toward the light. I'm conscious of the pain we're encroaching upon. I peer into grim expressions whose shadows bear resemblance to a mother who has lost a child. Eyes wounded. Voices weeping. Thoughts lost to grief.

"I'm sorry for your loss," I say to the troopers.

They lift a glance.

"I want you to come with me. To the crisis center."

"What for?" asks the state trooper with the leathery face.

"To help you deal with your loss."

Reticent, they trade glances with each other.

"I've gone through a session. Just finished taking classes. Trust me. You need this. It will help you get through this a lot easier. Help you to understand."

Heads lowered, they pause several beats.

"What time do you get off work?" I ask.

The leathery face glances at his watch. "Half an hour."

"I'll come and getcha. We'll drive to the crisis center together."

TWENTY-EIGHT

May 10, 1989 - 7:00 AM

I'm in bed. At the station. Random thoughts swim through the cobwebs of my mind.

I don't feel like getting up right now. Not just yet.

I think of the trooper we tried to save a couple of weeks ago, the memory pitted deep in my consciousness. Odd that he lived until we released him from the steering wheel. I wonder if he felt any pain. He didn't seem to display any outward signs. No yelling. No tears. He communicated with his eyes.

Whoort! Whoort!

"Channel Two. EMS. Rollover. Dysart and Indian School Roads. West Valley."

The muffled announcement cut into my thoughts. I listen for the assignment.

"Seventeen! Code three!" Al shouts.

I peel my face from the pillow. Rub the sleep from my eyes. I don the uniform. Slip into my work boots. Pull the zipper. Head out to meet Trevor. We get into the ambulance.

*****

May 10, 1989 – 7:07 AM

The dust is thick. Blue and red lights from a single patrol car flicker through the haze of fine dry particles. Bodies lie twisted on the narrow road where only two lanes of traffic traverse. Several more lie roadside. A black Suburban has settled into a ditch leaning at a forty-five-degree angle. The right front tire is missing, and the sheriff's deputy is busy pulling bodies out of the dented car.

"Call control. We're gonna need helicopters," I say.

I get out of the ambulance. Confiscate our gear. Head toward the first victim I see – a woman whose body lies on the westbound lane of the paved artery. The area west of the intersection at Dysart and Indian School is usually devoid of human existence. And that works in our favor today.

I throw the air bag to the ground, drop to a knee.

She's whimpering. Long black hair splattered with blood. Face scratched. A laceration above the eye. A smudge of dirt on her left cheek. Blood seeps through hands that are clenched to her stomach. I shift their position, moving her arms to her sides. Her frail face knots. A deep cut to the midsection reveals itself. Blood spills from her slender body.

"How are you doing?" I ask with a soothing tone.

Moist brown eyes pin mine. "My little girl." She winces. "Where's my little girl?"

I straighten her body, then her clothing.

"She's fine. Everything's going to be all right," I say. "You've got a pretty bad cut to your abdomen. I'm going to take your blood pressure, get an IV started, then I'm going to clean and bandage the cut. I'll have to rip open the skirt of your dress to do that, okay?"

"I gotta find my little girl."

"We'll find her and we'll take care of her."

I take her blood pressure. *Eighty over one twenty.*

She grimaces.

I prepare her arm for the IV.

Trevor approaches. "Took 'em a minute to understand we didn't have the manpower to handle the ten or more bodies we have lying out here. Told her we couldn't get another mobile unit out here fast enough to handle the call. They finally got it. They're sending five copters out now."

"Perfect."

Trevor glances in the direction of the Suburban. "I'm gonna go help the deputy."

I nod acknowledgment.

Trevor departs.

"I've got to know where my little girl is." Tears stream down the side of her face.

I insert the IV needle and secure it with medical tape.

I peer into eyes wounded with grief.

"It's going to be all right. We're going to find your little girl and we're going to take care of her just like we're taking care of you. But right now, we have to focus on you, okay? And I need your help. Can I count on you?"

I take her temperature. It's a hundred and two degrees. All normal for the trauma she's in.

"But, my baby," she whimpers. "I need to know she's okay. I need to know where she is."

"I understand, but there's only three of us right now. Help is on the way. We're doing everything we can. Everything is going to be okay."

I glance at her laceration.

"I'm going to cut the skirt open now and dress the wound."

I remove supplies from the airbag.

"What's your little girl's name?" I ask.

"Patty."

"Patty. What a pretty name."

I take an alcohol swab. Clean the area around the laceration.

"How old is she?"

"Five."

"As soon as I'm done here, I'll go look for Patty

and take care of her."

"Will you tell me when you find her?"

"If I can. We've got a lot of others to attend to."

I finish dressing the wound.

She nods acceptance.

"Just lie still until help comes, okay? I'll go find Patty."

" 'Kay."

I pick up the air bag and walk away.

I eye Trevor. He's hovered over a patient, peeling up eyelids. The sheriff's deputy, dressed in dark brown khaki pants with a tan-colored button-down shirt, throws a blanket over a body he has just removed from the Suburban. Trevor lifts a glance to me.

I cast about for the next victim.

A teenage boy lies curled on the road. A bone juts from the long sleeve of his western styled shirt, patterned in multiple shades of blue checkers. He bleeds from his nose and from the deep cut on his forehead. I drop to my knees and gently roll him to his back, taking care not to disrupt the bone. He lets out a soft grunt.

"Can you hear me?" I ask.

No response.

God. He's just a baby. Tears prick my eyes.

I prepare the oxygen mask and place it over his face. I hook up the oxygen tank and adjust oxygen levels.

I check his pulse. *Eighty-five over one hundred*

twenty.

I peel the lids of his eyes. Flash the penlight. Pupils narrow. *Good.*

I crane my neck to the sound of thumping blades in the distance.

I pull a blanket to shield me and the boy from the onslaught of dust that will soon infuse the air.

I swallow, working my throat as I clean up the bleeding and bandage the cuts. The sweet smell of fresh blood quickly fills our makeshift tent depositing the acrid scent of iron and dirt into my mouth.

I wince.

I prepare the boy's arm for splinting, cutting away the sleeve to clean the area around the jutting bone.

"Hurts," softly slips through his lips.

"I'm sorry," I say.

I apply cold packs to the area and place his arm on the arm board as comfortably as I can, securing it with medical tape.

I glimpse tears seeping through closed eyes.

I ratchet down a sinking feeling.

Throwing gusts of wind and shearing the quiet with the roar of their blades, helicopters land.

I prepare the IV.

The galloping of footsteps draw near.

I toss the blanket aside.

"Whatcha got?" a paramedic asks as she lays the backboard beside the boy.

I lift a look to a plain-looking petite female with

a brown pony tail tied to the back of her head. "Semi-conscious male with a compound fracture and lacerations to the head."

"Stabilized?"

"So far," I say.

"Let's roll 'im."

We roll the boy onto the backboard, careful not to jar the bone. We lift the backboard and run it to the helicopter. Return to treat the others.

I scan the landscape for Patty, eyeing a small figure in the distance.

I walk over to the red and black checkered dress lying on the side of the road, the body – twisted, the dark brown eyes – blank. I roil at the sight of her lifeless form.

The drone of an engine draws near. I dart a glance. It's the First Call vehicle – a black Chevy Suburban. I shake my head at the irony of it – the First Call vehicle being identical to the one involved in the crash.

Doors open for the deceased being carried to the car.

Helicopters lift off the ground to carry the injured away.

I lay a blue blanket next to Patty. I collect Patty into my arms and place her gently in the middle so that she is diagonal to the corners. I straighten her dress – pull her cadaverous eyes shut. I wrap the blanket to swaddle her as I would a baby.

"Whatcha got?" Trevor asks.

I give him a startled look.

His eyes narrow. "A kid?"

"Her name is Patty," I say.

"I'm sorry, Jimmy."

"Hey. It's life, right?" I say with a dispirited edge.

I cradle her in my arms – carry her to the opened doors of the black Suburban where the blue tarp awaits. I place her on the tarp, securing her in the same fashion as I did the blanket. I stare at the body of the little girl who will never know what her life might have been.

"We're about done here, Jimmy," says Trevor.

I scan the area. A wrecking crew is working the maimed Suburban. The landscape is absent people and helicopters. The sheriff's deputy is walking our way.

"Hey, guys. Thanks for your help."

"You bet," I say. "This was a bad one."

"Agreed." He waves a hand and hurries off.

"Let's go, Jimmy," Says Trevor. "I'll let them know we're available."

TWENTY-NINE

May 10, 1989 – 11:28 AM

The steady drone of trundling tires bites into a pervading stillness that encumbers the drive back to the station.

I turn on the radio. A commercial announcing an upcoming rock concert breaches the quiet. I turn the dial searching for music.

"That was some call," Trevor provides.

I answer him with a soft nod and a "Yup."

I stumble onto *Sweet Child of Mine* by Guns N Roses. Satisfied, I leave the dial in place.

"You know, some calls don't require an effort to be compassionate and to treat people better when administering care," Trevor says. "This was one of them."

I arch an eyebrow. "Since when do you care about compassion and treating people better?"

Trevor squints. "I don't know, Jimmy. I'm just saying."

I let the comment drop. Settle myself into the seat. Hum to the music while Trevor guides the ambulance.

"You'd have to be one cold bastard not to show compassion on a call like this one. Even Joe couldn't be that cruel," says Trevor.

"You're kidding, right? Joe don't give a shit about nothing other than his daughter. He couldn't treat a patient with compassion if you gave him step by step instructions."

Trevor laughs. "Still."

I lower the volume on the radio.

"So what's got you all interested in compassion and treating people better?" I ask.

"Nothing, really. It's just that... well... I've been watching you."

"Watching me?"

"Yeah."

"Watching me what?"

"Watching you work. Your change in attitude. I mean, I see you really working at it. I don't know. I guess I didn't realize how serious you were."

I lower my gaze. "Yeah, well."

"Jimmy, I think what you are doing is phenomenal."

"Really?"

"Yeah. I see the effort you put into caring for people. I'm amazed by what you're accomplishing."

"I don't know what to say."

"You don't have to say anything, but seriously, you've got me feeling optimistic."

"You? Optimistic?" I chuckle. "Optimistic about what?"

"I don't know. How about the future?"

"Optimistic about the future. Hmmm." I rub my chin. "I'm starting to worry about you, Trevor," I say with jest.

Trevor snorts a chuckle. "Why?"

"All this talk about compassion and shit." We round a corner. "But seriously. I really do appreciate the acknowledgment. It gives me hope and encouragement."

"Well, you deserve it. I've come to admire what you are trying to do," says Trevor. "You're a sight bigger person than I will ever be."

Warm emotion spreads through me, filling me with gratitude. I cast an appreciative look Trevor's way. "Naw, man. Never bigger. We are all growing."

"Whatever."

Silence.

"So how's your training with Sam coming along?"

"Terrific. Learning a lot."

"Yeah?"

"You remember that rollover we had a couple weeks ago in Maricopa? The one where the officer was pinned by the steering wheel?"

"Sure do."

"Those guys were my first case."

"How do you mean?"

"Sam actually let me handle that one on my own. I mean he hung around to moderate, but he let me take the lead. Debrief the troopers."

"Yeah?"

I exhale a stream of air. "Man. I was scared."

"Why?"

"Cuz I didn't know what I was doing."

"You took the course. Passed the test, didn't ya?"

"Yeah. But I didn't have any hands-on experience other than the time *I* was the trauma victim."

"Well, how'd you do?"

"Good." I smile pausing a beat. "They're like a brotherhood, those guys. You have no idea the impact a trauma like that has on the brotherhood. These guys take that shit pretty hard."

"I could imagine. It's just like us, right?"

"Something like that. Maybe from a different angle given the fact that their personal life is always on the line."

"Hmmm. You might have a point."

Trevor makes a right turn onto Glendale Avenue where traffic flows a little heavier.

"It felt so good to be able to do something to actually help someone instead of *wishing* I could help." I spot our favorite Italian restaurant as we drive by. "We did some good work on those guys. I learned a lot. Couldn't have done it without Sam, though. He is definitely God sent."

"Oh. I bet you could have," Trevor says with a tacit knowing.

"Could have what?"

"Done it without Sam."

"I don't know," I say with an air of doubt. "He had to jump in a few times."

"So?" Trevor pulls up to a stoplight. "And Sam must be something special for you to like him so much."

I reach down to unzip my boots. "He is."

"Engine Seventeen" peals from the radio. "Man down. Ninety-two Twenty-Three North Fourteenth Drive. Code three."

"Figures," I say.

Trevor lifts the mic. I re-zip my boots. We turn the ambulance around.

*****

May 10, 1989 – 12:49 PM

We arrive at a residential home. The door opens. I catch the eye of a tired-looking matronly woman in her late fifties. She's dressed in a red loose-fitting swing dress cinched at the waist. Her short salt and pepper hair is held in place with a head band. Earrings glisten. "This way," she says with a hurried tone.

We enter the foyer. I glance at the man standing

in front of the fireplace. He's middle aged – maybe mid-forties. Silver hair. Wire-rimmed glasses. Navy-blue business suit with a white button-down dress shirt. He stands with hands clasped at his hips speaking to a group of about fifty people. His projection is poor. Scattered words on immigration and victim's rights bounce off my ears.

"What's going on?" I ask the matron.

"Fundraiser for a candidate running for some political office."

"Ah," I reply.

We're shouldered to the back of the crowd where the entry way to the kitchen sections off the main living area. The victim is seated on the floor. Back against the wall. Legs spread into a V. Surrounded by a handful of people who stare at him as though he's an anomaly.

I check his vitals.

Trevor stoops to meet the man's gaze. He's semi-conscious. Head lolling. Eyes unfocused behind black-framed glasses. He smiles revealing jagged teeth.

"How are you doing?" Trevor asks while readying the oxygen mask.

"I'm okay. Just a little light headed," the man replies. "I'll be okay."

"I know you will," Trevor says with a soothing tone. "We're going to take care of you anyway. Take you to the hospital. Just to be sure."

I cast a look to Trevor surprised by the elevated

level of care he seems to have undertaken.

I prepare the IV. "How are you feeling?" I ask peering into the patient's eyes.

"All this trouble for a little lightheadedness," the patient replies.

I smile.

"I'm going to place this mask over your face to make sure you're getting enough oxygen and to make breathing easier for you," Trevor informs the patient.

Trevor gently positions the oxygen mask. "There. How does that feel?"

"Fine," he replies with muted tone.

Trevor adjusts the oxygen.

"You comfortable?" Trevor asks.

He nods.

"I'm going to insert the IV needle," I say to the patient. "You will feel a little pin prick. Shouldn't hurt too bad," I add with a smile.

The patient nods an acknowledgment.

I insert the needle. Tape it in place. Shoot a quick glance to the patrons attuned to the speaker. *Fifty people here and not one person has bothered to acknowledge a medical emergency is taking place*. I'm stunned with disbelief.

"We're going to lift you to the gurney now," says Trevor in a gentle tone.

I dart a second glance to Trevor not quite sure I'm actually witnessing the level of care he seems to have engaged in.

We lift the patient. Secure him to the gurney. Roll him out the front door. The matron follows. Two others trail her. "Will he be all right?" she asks.

"I'm sure he'll be fine," I say.

We load him into the ambulance. Take him to Saint Rita's.

*****

May 10, 1989 – 2:12 PM

We pull into the driveway of the hospital's emergency access. Unload the patient. Take him to the emergency room.

Mary greets us at the door.

"Hey, Jimmy. Trevor. Whadda we got?"

The patient turns his gaze to Mary. "I'm fine, really. Just a little light headed." His speech muffled by the oxygen mask.

"Looks like he temporarily lost consciousness," I say.

"Okay. Let's get him checked out," she says.

The medical team rolls the patient into the ER. Transfers him to hospital equipment. Begins treatment.

"C'mon. I'll take the report," Mary says. We walk with her to the nurses' station. She casts a brief look my way. "I hear you're a Certified Critical Incident Stress Debriefer now, Jimmy. That true?"

"Yup," I say adding a broad smile.

"Is it everything you thought it would be?" she

asks with a grin.

"And more," I say. "Do you see my eyes twinkling with pride?" I give a quick grin. "I just love working with Sam. He's so knowledgeable. Patient, too. I don't believe I've ever met anyone with that kind of patience."

"Like I've said in the past, Jimmy, Sam's a good man."

"Yeah. He is," I say with a tone of reflection.

Mary collects the patient's file. "Let's get the report done and over with."

Trevor recounts the evening's event. Mary takes notes. I stand idly by surveying the emergency room.

A doctor walks towards me. His white medical jacket melds with the white walls of the hospital. He wears a black stethoscope draped around his neck.

"Looks like your guy is going to be all right," he says.

"What was it?" I ask.

"Low blood sugar."

"That's it?"

"That's it," the doctor repeats. "He's got his instructions. Family is on the way."

I nod.

"Thanks for the help, Doc."

"That's my job," he says. "Listen, guys. I gotta run. Duty calls."

I raise two fingers in mock salute. The doctor departs.

I turn my attention to Trevor and Mary. "We about finished with the report?"

"Yes," Trevor says.

"I'll head to the ambulance. Let them know we're available."

"Okay. I'm right behind you," Trevor says.

THIRTY

We're driving to the station. Talking about Mary. Recounting scenes from the call. The radio blisters. "Seventeen. Man down, Corner of Seventh Street and Palmaire. Code three."

I pull the mic from its pocket. Trevor turns the ambulance. We race to the scene.

Two firemen hover over a man who is seated listlessly on the ground, his body limp.

We get out of the ambulance. Walk up to the firemen. They're laughing. Making obscene gestures.

I eye the victim. He's unconscious. Legs sprawled, head lolling about on his chest, drool streaming from his mouth.

"What's so funny?" I ask as I scan the victim's body. His white tee shirt smudged with dirt doesn't quite cover the beer belly that extends beyond his belt. Tatty blue jeans stretched from overuse. Short brown hair matted and sweaty. The beginnings of a beard shadows his face.

"Look at this fool." The fireman with wavy hair responds. "He's drunk."

"Yeah," I say as I glean a look at the patient's face. "What's that in his nostrils?"

"Smelling salts," wavy hair gives a quick short laugh. "We broke the capsules. Shoved them up his nose just for yuks."

"That's pure ammonia carbonate," I grimace. "You know what that will do to his nostrils?"

"Yeah," the other fireman who is bald and square-jawed sneers.

Trevor rushes to the victim. Drops into a crouch. Pulls the capsules from his nose.

"Awww. Whadja do that for?" wavy hair whines.

"Cuz I'm not a dick," Trevor says.

I catch Trevor's eye. Read the tacit understanding between us. He has joined my cause.

"Who you callin' a dick?" wavy hair snarls.

We meet the question with silence. I drop to my knees. Join Trevor to treat the patient.

"Ah, c'mon. Let's have a little fun with him," the bald one goads.

"He's so drunk he won't have a clue," says wavy hair.

"You guys are idiots," I say as I place the oxygen mask over the patient's face.

"We're the idiots?" wavy hair says. "How insulting."

I crane my neck. Remind myself to be unconditional. I say it anyway. "Do you even know what the word means?"

"Fuck you," he replies.

I give a sharp look.

"Hand me the pen light, Trevor."

"C'mon Jake. Let's get outta here. Leave these two pussies to clean up this mess." The bald one takes a step. "Oh look." Wavy hair lifts an arm. Points to the drunk. "He's vomiting." Both break into laughter.

I press my lips. Glare at them. "I thought you were leaving."

Wavy hair winks. "We are. Wouldn't want to miss this though. This is better than I anticipated."

Trevor stands. Clenches his fists. Walks over to fireman with the wavy hair. Stands on his tip toes. Gets into his face. "Fuck off."

Wavy hair snorts a laugh. Backs away. They get into their vehicle. Start the engine. Laughter echoes as they drive off.

"Bastards!" I yell. "Mother fuckers ought to have a cattle prod shoved up their ass."

"You got that right," Trevor says.

"I just don't get it, Trevor. How can anybody be so mean to someone who cannot defend himself."

"They're cowards, Jimmy. You see how they backed down?"

"Yeah. Still. I oughta report 'em."

"What good would it do? Nothing will be done about it anyway."

"Ah, you're right." I let out a small guttural groan.

"Help me with this guy, will ya?" Trevor says. We clean up the patient. Load him onto the gurney. Put him in the back of the ambulance.

"At least I remembered to be somewhat unconditional," I say to Trevor.

"I noticed that."

"That's right. You're watching me," I chuckle.

"You got that right." Trevor laughs.

"C'mon. Let's get him to the hospital," I say.

THIRTY-ONE

May 17, 1989 – 4:00 PM

It's been slow today. A couple of calls. Ambulances are maintained. Utility room stocked. Station cleaned. We sit at the table in the kitchenette. *Emergency!* flickers from the television monitor. Dennis and Mark play backgammon. Steve and Bill are out on an errand. Four of us play poker. The rest of the crew is off today.

I take a sip of soda.

Trevor eyes the hand he's been dealt. Strategically pulls two cards. Tosses them to the table. "I'll take two."

Joe deals the two cards.

"What about you, Ace."

"Gimme three," Al says.

Joe deals. Al collects the cards. Folds them into his hand.

"Mandy's graduating pretty soon, isn't she?" asks Dennis.

"Yeah. Next week," Joe says – his arrogance on full display.

My stomach clenches. I hate working with Joe. Hate playing cards with him, too. He's such a crude ass.

He nods to me with a 'how many?'

"Did you get 'er her car yet?" Dennis asks.

"Yup. Sure did. Gave it to her about a week ago."

"Your roll, Dennis," Mark says.

A shaking of the dice. They tumble to the board.

"How's she liking it?"

"Loves it." Joe places the cards on the table. Pulls out his wallet. "Here. I have a picture."

He hands it to me. I briefly eye the young beauty with long dark hair draped over her shoulders. Her dark eyes twinkle. A broad smile stretches across her face. She leans against the forest green Ford club coupe with the distinctive ponton styling – a rounded flowing form with a bulbous slab-sided configuration that was very popular in its day. So were the white wall tires. I nod. Pass the picture to Dennis.

I shuffle my feet. Lift a glance around. "Can we get back to the game?"

"Give it a minute," Joe says. He takes a drink of soda.

Al hands Joe the picture. "Nice, huh?" Joe says.

"Yeah," all agree.

Joe puts the picture back into his wallet.

"She's up in Flagstaff. Wanted to show off her car at the Classic Auto Show they're runnin' up there."

"Yeah?" Dennis says.

"Yup. Her and a couple of friends. They're coming back tonight."

Joe collects his cards. "You're up Jimmy."

I throw down a card. "Gimme one." Eyeing the cards in my hand, I concentrate on the king I need to make two pair hoping to will it into existence.

"You sure, Jimmy, because you can't change your mind once I deal the card."

"I know that, Joe." My voice taking on an edge. "Just gimme the card."

Joe tosses the card on the table.

"You got big plans for her graduation?" Dennis continues.

"We're renting a couple of rooms at the Pointe. Gonna spend the weekend there."

"Yeah?" says Dennis.

"Got the entertainment set up and everything. You know. For her and her friends," Joe adds.

"Sounds mighty expensive to me," Mark mumbles. He rolls the dice.

"Where do you get the money for all this Joe?" asks Trevor.

"You ever hear of a second mortgage?" Joe responds.

"You're gonna get yourself in some serious financial trouble if you keep spending like this." I collect the card.

"Don't you worry about me, Jimmy," Joe says.

I glance at the card. Exhale a heavy breath. Fold it into my hand anyway. "Trust me. I'm not."

Joe gives a hard look.

"I bet a quarter," says Trevor who holds a look of confidence in his expression.

"I call," says Al. He throws a quarter into the pot.

Joe tosses his quarter.

"I fold."

"Read 'em and weep," Trevor says. He spreads his kings and eights for everyone to see. "Full house."

"Dawg," Al says. He throws his cards to the table. Leans back in his chair. Clasps his hands behind his head.

"You cheated," Joe says.

"No. I. didn't." Trevor protests.

Scraping his chair across the floor, Joe rises and walks to the great room.

Trevor pats his belly. "I'm hungry. Let's get something to eat."

"I'm all for that," I say while rubbing my eyes.

"Where do you want to go?" asks Al.

"Oh, let's just go to that little Mexican restaurant up the street. It's walking distance." Trevor says.

"Sounds good," says Al.

They rise from the table. "Joe. You comin'?" asks Dennis.

Whoort! Whoort!

"Chanel Two. EMS assignment. Rollover accident. I-17 and New River. Engine Twelve."

"Figures," Trevor says as he casts a downward look.

Al answers the phone. "Station Eleven."

A pause.

"All units. Code three," he adds.

*****

May 17, 1989 – 5:20 PM

The roar of the hurst tool echoes off canyon walls. Chunks of metal squeal in retaliation to the violent assault. A small red fire truck is parked along the edge of the road, a squad car parked behind.

We get out of our vehicles, jog with our equipment to the crest of the highway. I eye the wreckage below. The car rests on its rooftop amidst the desert landscape of burnt Joshua trees, rotted cacti, overgrown parcels of green shrubbery and dead grass. Firemen work to remove bodies. A deputy is taking notes. Another walks the scene. We break formation, start down the slope when Joe suddenly stops. I nearly run into him. "What the fuck, Joe."

My comment is met with an eerie silence.

"Joe." I say with sharp tone.

He turns to me. I register a blend of terror and shock.

"What's wrong?"

Mouth opens. Lips work. No words come out.

"What is it, Joe?" I say with alarm.

He lifts an arm. Points to the wreckage.

I shift my gaze.

"What?"

A hoarse whisper. "The car."

I study the crumpled metal with a rounded hood and white wall tires. The color could easily be black, but a closer look reveals dust and debris veiling what could just as easily be a forest green.

Can't be.

Joe gathers his senses. Breaks into a run. "Maanndeee!" The shrilling cry penetrates my soul.

I run behind Joe. The rest of the crew is already working. Joe lurches toward the car. The hurst tool lifts. The motor dies. I stop short. All eyes are now on Joe. A "what the fuck" cuts into the commotion.

"Mandee!" A terrible wail bounces off canyon walls.

Muscles bulge. Jaw tightens. Lips press. Face stiffens. He works. With blinded focus and an unnatural strength Joe takes hold of the driver's door, lets out a primal roar and rips the door from its hinges. He tosses the obstacle to the ground. "Mandee!" he shrills.

He reaches into the driver's side. Removes his

daughter. Cradles her in his arms. "Mandy. Mandy. Mandy. Mandy," he cries. He steps away from the car. Lowers himself to the ground. Caressing her face, he weeps. "My baby girl. Whadja do?" He stops. Tilts his chin. Opens his mouth. A silent scream. Tears stream.

Rooted in our positions, we stare dumbfounded – in quiet disbelief.

Trevor glances at me. A question of "what do we do?" planted in his expression.

I shrug my shoulders.

Joe weeps. Caresses her face frantically. Feigns combing her hair. Cries awful sobs.

I clench my jaw. Walk over to Trevor. Al, Dennis, and Mark join me. "Let's get the rest of the victims taken care of. I'll keep an eye on Joe."

They nod. Work with the remaining victims. Firemen and deputies follow suit.

I eye the man whose arrogance has just been reduced to a submission to God. A pleading for life. His head arches back. He cries out spasms of pain as he holds his daughter tight, rocking her as if to rock her back to life.

I bite back a tempting thought. Think better of it. *No one deserves this.*

The canyon echoes a terrible wail of despair. His body quakes.

I look away, a question pulling at my thoughts.

How are we going to peel him from his daughter?

I cast a look around as if searching for an answer.

"We're about done," Trevor says as he approaches from behind. He takes a breath and darts a glance to Joe. "What are we going to do about him?"

I exhale a sigh. "I don't know," I answer levelly.

Dusk is approaching. A soft breeze eases my tension.

I glance at Al. His expression carries the same question. I meet his gaze with a look of resignation. "We've got to separate him from his daughter."

I turn a glance to Mark and Dennis who are walking toward us. Read the question in their eyes.

"Mandy's dead. I don't think he's accepting that yet," I say to the group.

"That's gonna make it extra tough," says Al.

I nod agreement.

The two deputies approach, their expressions grim. "You need help?" They nod at Joe.

A firefighter interrupts. "I told the First Call vehicle to wait for her. Let them know what's going on." He eyes Joe. "You're gonna need help with him."

I cast a glance to Joe, then back to the fireman.

"Agreed."

I turn to the deputy. "Yes. We'll need your help."

*****

May 17, 1989 – 6:39 PM

The five of us drop to our knees. We surround Joe. Firefighters and deputies stand to the side. A grave hollowness seizes me.

"Joe," I say hesitantly. "It's time to go."

A bitter dare pins my gaze. Snot lingers on his upper lip. Nose red. Eyes bulging. Face swollen. "I'm not leaving her."

The five of us trade glances. "Joe," I say. "We need to take care of Mandy. It's time for us to go."

"No!" he yells with an intensity that emanates from the core of his gut.

"If you don't let her go willingly, we will have to take her by force."

"I. Dare. You." He challenges.

"Look, Joe. I know how hard this is on you already. Please. Don't make it any harder than it already has to be," I plead.

I'm met with a sudden deep guttural cry as though something evil has taken over. "I can't, Jimmy. I can't let her go," he sobs convulsive sobs.

We rise. Wait several beats. Give the firemen and deputies a nod of approval.

I cast a downward look. "I'm so sorry, Joe."

The firemen lean in. Joe takes a swing with a fisted hand. His face a look of rage. "You're. Not. Taking. My. daughter. You fucks!" He chokes through savage tears.

He rolls to shield Amanda. A fireman takes hold of an arm. Joe easily breaks free. Rolls to his back.

284

Takes a swing. The fireman jumps back. Realizing he's at a disadvantage, Joe sits up. Scoots his back up against a solid piece of the car taking Amanda with him. We make another attempt to secure his arms. All four firefighters work together as Joe swings wildly with the right arm, holding Amanda with his left. They collar his arm. Hold him down. Joe kicks, fighting the entrapment that weakens his hold on Amanda. I nod a look to Al then to the arm. Al elbows Mark. Mark reads the understanding. Dennis follows suit. Joe fires back with a hard hold and another kick allowing his right arm to succumb to the entrapment. He tries to upend himself. The two deputies respond. Secure his legs. His body twists again with an effort to break free. Joe yells obscenities I'm not sure I've heard before, his feral tone frightening. I jump in to help.

Battling his strength, we break Amanda free. Eight men struggle to hold Joe back. Al and I collect Amanda.

"Mandeee!" Joe howls an awful sound as he fights to break free.

We try to shield her from Joe's view. Lay her on the blanket. Fold it over her.

"Don't you cover her in that blanket," Joe roils. "She's. Not. Dead."

I lift a gaze. Catch his expression. He weeps a resignation. Lowers his head.

"My Mandy," he cries softly. "My baby girl," he weeps.

We carry her to the First Call vehicle. Place her on the blue tarp. I gaze at the lifeless form that has forever changed her father's life.

"C'mon, Jimmy."

Al and I roll her. We close the door. Signal completion with a quick fist to the back of the car.

THIRTY-TWO

May 17, 1989 – 7:59 PM

Trevor guides the ambulance back to the station. I sit on the bench beside Joe in the patient's cabin. The vibration of trundling tires shimmies through the base of my spine while thoughts swirl on the best way to open a dialogue. I chance an approach.

"Joe."

His face is drawn. Hands clasped. A sorrowful expression dials down to the floorboard.

I breathe.

"Joe."

A pause.

"Tell me what happened, Joe. Tell me what you saw."

Red, moist eyes rise slowly. I hand him a tissue. He blows his nose. "You were there, Jimmy. You saw what happened."

I turn to face him. "Not from your point of view, Joe." I catch his eye. Speak with a soothing tone. "Walk me through the scene."

He lowers his head. The corners of his mouth arch downward. Lips quiver. His voice breaks. "I can't, Jimmy."

I place my hand on his shoulder. "You have to. For Mandy's sake."

He gives his head a hard shake. "She's dead."

"I know." I pause for a silent moment. "She wouldn't want you holding this in. Suffering the way you're suffering. Tell me what happened."

A tear drops to his lap. He swipes at his eyes.

"Joe."

He lifts his head. Stares into space.

"The car." His voice trembles. "The first thing I noticed was the car." He pauses, casting a downward look. "And I knew she was dead. I could tell by the way the car had landed. And there was a knowing that injected itself into me. Like a ghoul had taken possession." He inhales a stream of air. Releases it slowly. "But I refused to believe it. Threw that thought right out the window of my mind. Convinced myself she was alive."

He wrings his hands. More tears. He sniffles them back.

I lean my forearms on my knees. "Go on, Joe. What happened next?"

His moist eyes flicker. "I really don't know."

I take a beat. "Think, Joe." I shift my position.

"It's really important."

He searches his mind. Runs trembling fingers through his hair. Takes a deep breath. "I felt the strength of something mighty infuse itself into me. My body stiffened. Felt like cement. My mind went blank. Like I passed out or something. The next thing I remember is holding Mandy in my arms. Smoothing her hair. Wiping the blood off her face." He casts a glance to blood stained hands.

"You don't remember ripping the door off its hinges?"

"No." His eyes throw a question. "I did that?"

"Yeah."

He turns away. "I don't remember."

He picks at his fingers.

"Go on," I say. "What happened next?"

He takes a bite of fingernail. Spits it out. Clasps his hands. "I refused to acknowledge the gash in her forehead. Her crushed cheek bone. The ground in dirt on her face. In my mind's eye, they didn't exist. But they were there. Every bit of them. And the cuts and bruises stared back at me. Mocking me. As if to say, 'Pay attention, you idiot. Your daughter is dead.' I refused to, Jimmy. I refused to accept the fact my baby was dead."

He pauses a few beats. Lifts a sorrowful look. "Her teeth were missing, Jimmy. I just couldn't accept that. Her beautiful smile – gone." He cups his face and weeps.

A familiar gnawing of pain encroaches upon me.

I blink.

"She's dead, Jimmy!" he cries out. "I'll never hold her again. Never touch her. Never laugh with her again. I'll never have another opportunity to look into her beautiful brown eyes." He pauses. "I didn't even get a chance to tell her how much I love her." He rounds his shoulders. His body quakes.

A distant memory. Pooling like an oil spill. Filling my core with a hard raw ache.

"She's gone, Jimmy. I loved her so much. And I don't know what to do." He sobs.

A corrosive void. Of something lost. The essence of which cannot be described in words. An intimacy. Violated. Like a wounded animal. It claws at my flesh.

I ratchet down the agony.

"What else, Joe."

"I remember someone trying to take her from me. Pulling her out of my arms. I fought to keep her. Didn't want to let her go." He sobs. "And then they took her from me, Jimmy." He lifts a look. Catches my eye. "You took her from me."

I exhale a heavy breath.

"I had to, Joe. You know I had to."

"I know," Joe concedes.

I look deep into his eyes. Ensconced in his torture I dissolve into the trenchant emptiness. An evisceration of the soul. The remains of a deep dark cavity.

A strong desire to cry ratchets up. My eyes

moisten. I push the pain back. Focus on Joe.

"How did you feel, Joe?"

"What do you mean, how did I feel? How do you think I felt."

I sit back. Hands resting to the side of me. "It's not about what I think, Joe. It's about how you feel."

I struggle with my own emotional stronghold. The gritting penetration. The chasm in the body. The desecration of the soul. "What I think doesn't matter. It's what you perceive that matters here. Only you can relay how you feel. How it affects you. I can only interpret what I see through the veil of my own experience. Not yours. Your experience is different."

Joe nods acceptance. His expression stolid.

"How did you feel?"

He mates his fingers. Steeples his thumbs. "Like being tortured alive."

"What does that mean?"

He pauses to search his mind. "Like acid burning my insides. Like being burned alive on the inside." He casts a gaze to the floorboard.

I imagine the feeling. It merges with the memory. The deleterious desolation that comes from the inability to engage. A muted guttural cry releases from deep inside me. Tears prick my eyes. I push them back. My thoughts return to Joe.

"Why do you think you feel that way?"

I read his expression. It's weighted with a

question: *"Are you some special kind of stupid?"*

"Because she's gone, Jimmy. She's gone from my existence. Never to return. We'll never enjoy a meal together. Go to the lake. The fair. Swimming. All the things fathers do with their daughters. I'll never be able to do them again with her or her children." He rounds his shoulders. Sobs. Then continues, "I'll never meet my grandchildren. Never get to be the grandfather I dreamed of being. Never get to experience the joys of having a family. My family has been ripped from my existence. Do you understand that?"

A familiar feeling of emptiness causes tears to well once again. I pluck several tissues. Hand one to Joe.

"I do." We weep.

"Why you crying, Jimmy?"

"I know the hurt. I feel it in you."

"You've lost someone?"

"Not to death. It was a long time ago."

He nods an understanding.

"Do you have family you can call?" I ask.

"A brother."

"Let's give him a shout when we get to the station."

THIRTY-THREE

July 28, 1989 – 1:58 AM

It's 1:58 AM. I'm home. In bed. Can't sleep. My mind's awhirl.

It's been a couple of months since the passing of Joe's daughter. The memory haunts me as surely as a specter looms.

I exhale a long stream of air. Run my fingers through my hair. Sink into the abyss of that terrible tragedy.

The crushing of the heart, the crippling of the soul, the eternal chasm I imagine is pitted deep into the center of his chest.

I sit up in bed. Turn on the light. Pad to the kitchen to get a bottle of beer.

I stayed with Joe for two days following that terrible accident. Spent most of the time on the sofa in his living room. Talking. Reminiscing. Hurting.

He spoke of the many times he took her to Disneyland, Magic Mountain, the California beaches. He talked of her favorite ride. Told how she would squeal when the roller coaster would crash into the water. Spoke of her athletic abilities, too. How she loved basketball. Baseball. Volleyball. And he loved to watch her play. We talked of his impending loneliness – the grief he would endure. Then he remembered a time when her mother was sad.

Mandy was eight years old, and she wanted to make her mom happy, let her know she was loved. So she took a can of white spray paint and painted Home Sweet Home on the forest green wall in the living room. I laughed while imagining the look of surprise on Joe's face as he described the words forming fine white lines that crawled down the wall till they pooled on the floor. Joe said he was so angry with Mandy, but he held his tongue. "What good would it do to yell at her now?" he said then. He chuckled at the memory. Then wept. I wept with him.

I walk back to the bedroom. Place the bottle of beer on the nightstand. Crawl into bed. I sit with my back against the headboard, my knees bent up to my chest. I take a swig of beer.

So hard to think all of us are back to work again like business as usual. Just another day. Another dollar. Except for Joe. He moved back to Michigan to be with his brother.

I remember the box of pictures. How he reminisced as we poured through them – one by one – telling story after story about her and the many things they did together. He'd chuckle. Weep. Then sob. I sat by his side. Placed a hand on his shoulder. Wept and sobbed with him.

I lean my head back.

Mary flashes to mind. *"Tell your stories."*

I reach into the night stand. Take a note pad and a pen.

I write the words, "tell your stories."

My thoughts turn to Joe. His sorrow. The worst day of his life.

Did I make a difference?

Then I warm to a memory of Trevor. *"You've got me feeling optimistic."* I smile. Write the word, "Optimistic."

And he taught me to use the word, unconditional, too. I take a swig of beer. Blindly place the bottle back on the night stand. Write the word, "Unconditional."

Of all people that I could have helped in my lifetime, Joe was the last person on this planet I would have ever figured I'd lend a hand to. I hated him. Yet I couldn't bear to see him in the tragedy he was entrenched in. It triggered my own memories. Regenerated old feelings. The ripping apart of my internal world. Like the savage bloodletting of a heartless vampire.

I shiver. There is a troubling sense of vulnerability connected to an incident that could crush a man like Joe. Crush a man like me.

So I helped him. Or at least I tried. Not really sure I made a difference.

I doodle. Move the words around on my note pad. Unconditional. Tell your story. Optimistic.

And what was the other word Mary planted in my brain?

I lift a gaze to the ceiling.

Oh yeah. Caring.

I write the word on my note pad, shortening it to "care."

Unconditional. Tell your story. Optimistic. Care. I eye the words speculatively.

I remember when the brother arrived, his face laden with grief. Joe introduced us. I shook his hand then gave him a manly hug. Informed them they would be in my prayers and that I would touch base from time to time to make sure they were good, adding that they should reach out to me if they needed my help. The brother folded to the door. I drifted to my truck.

I remember getting into the truck. Pausing a moment. Reflecting.

It felt good to help someone.

I pause my thoughts. Feel the feeling. I take a drink of beer and make a decision.

I want to help people.

Why?

I search my mind for an answer.

I really don't know. Maybe it's because of the time my father went out of his way on a Christmas morning to help a family with their firewood.

I remember the wood was wet and it wouldn't burn so they called my dad to make it right. True to his nature, my dad loaded our personal stock of dry wood into the brown Ford pickup truck and took me with him. "There's a lot of power to be had in helping people," my dad would say as I protested. "Personal power." He would pause. *"People need help, son. It feels good to help people. It makes you feel powerful."*

Not only did we deliver the wood, but Dad started the fire. I was so mad at him. I was ten, maybe eleven years old. I didn't care about power, personal or otherwise. Nor did I care about helping people. I wanted to ride my brand new ten speed bright red Radio Flyer bicycle I got for Christmas that morning.

I take another swig of beer.

Maybe that's where I got it from – my desire to help people. His words did seem to stick in my mind.

I write the words on my notepad. Power and Help.

I eye the words again. Move the pen around. Extract the first letter of the words.

U. T. O. C. P. H.

I see something here.

I shuffle the letters around. C. O. U. *What?*

I think. *What do I do with T. P. and H. C.O.U.T.H.?* I pause. *No. I need an extra C in there.*

P. O. U. C. H.

Power.

Optimistic.

Unconditional.

Care.

Help.

Let's see. You get power when you're optimistic, unconditional, caring and helping people.

I mull over the sense of it, not really warming to the message.

And what do I do with the T?

I evaluate the possibilities.

Naw. Trash that.

Wait!

I switch out the P for the T.

T.O.U.C. H.

A surge of warmth presses through my body. A smile unfolds naturally.

Tell your stories.

Optimistic.

Unconditional.

Care.

Help.

But what do I do with the P?

My dad's words flash to my mind. *There's a lot of power to be had in helping people. Personal power.*

Then it hits me like a brick to the head. *That's where your power lies.*

The words unfold. *To help others is to engage with them unconditionally, to encourage optimism and to show you genuinely care by going the extra mile.*

A giddy feeling shimmies through me.

When you tell your stories, are optimistic, are unconditional in your approach, and genuinely care about people, this helps people and it touches their lives in ways you can never know. That's power. That's...

THE

POWER

Of

T

O

U

C

H